The
DNAgers

Avon Books are available at special quantity discounts for bulk purchases for sales promotions, premiums, fund raising or educational use. Special books, or book excerpts, can also be created to fit specific needs.

For details write or telephone the office of the Director of Special Markets, Avon Books, Dept. FP, 1350 Avenue of the Americas, New York, New York 10019, 1-800-238-0658.

The DNAgers

STEVE and TERRY ENGLEHART

AN AVON CAMELOT BOOK

The DNAgers is an original publication of Avon Books. This work has never before appeared in book form.

AVON BOOKS
A division of
The Hearst Corporation
1350 Avenue of the Americas
New York, New York 10019

First Avon Camelot Printing: January 1997

CAMELOT TRADEMARK REG. U.S. PAT. OFF. AND IN OTHER COUNTRIES, MARCA REGISTRADA, HECHO EN U.S.A.

Printed in the U.S.A.

OPM 10 9 8 7 6 5 4 3 2 1

Thanks to
Annalee Rejhon and Joseph Duggan
for the medieval French poem

The
DNAgers

One

CUTTING SHARPLY TO HIS LEFT, JACK CHAMNESS INTER-cepted the ball, successfully taking control again for his team. With the score tied two-two and thirty seconds to go in this final game of the state soccer tournament, there was no time left for mistakes. Jack skillfully drib-bled around two lunging opponents and, with adrenaline rushing, shot a lightning pass to the Raptors' center forward. *Bam!* Into the goal just before the final whistle! The fans exploded in ecstatic cheers as they poured onto the muddy field to congratulate their team.

"You did it!" Jack's twin sister, Mary, squealed as she hugged her happily panting brother.

"Cool under pressure. That's our Jack!" their fa-ther exclaimed.

Their mother kissed his cheek and ruffled his hair. "You looked terrific out there, son!"

"Somebody had to do it," Jack said with his ragged grin. He always wanted the ball when he was on the field, but afterward, any personal glory embarrassed him. Too bad. When the trophies were presented ten

1

minutes later, Jack was named the tournament's Most Valuable Player.

"I wish you'd been a boy, sis," he told Mary as the camera flashes were still echoing visually behind their green eyes. "Then we might have been identical twins, and I could have sent you up on the podium."

"I like this arrangement just fine," answered Mary with mock disdain. "Who would want to look like you, let alone be a boy?"

Jack smiled at her; she was the one person he always liked to be around. A few strands of her straight auburn hair had escaped the ponytail she was wearing, and her clear eyes laughed behind her wire-rimmed glasses, as they usually did. Jack's wavy hair was light brown, and he had perfect vision. Each of the thirteen-year-old twins had a dimple, but on opposite cheeks. Both twins were athletic, but Mary's firm muscles were packed into a much more compact body, and she preferred orienteering and mountain biking to team sports. Oddly enough, she was the more social of the two; Jack was a team player, where there was little time for personal reflection.

Eventually the hero-worshiping played itself out, and the family was able to go home. They lived in a spacious apartment on the third floor of the city's history museum, where their father was the curator; and one thing about a museum, it was always quiet. Jack collapsed into bed immediately after dinner. Sleep washed over him, and sweet dreams of future World Cup triumphs filled his night.

*   *   *

"Wake up, sleepyhead! Even soccer stars have to go to school." Jack's father gave him a playful poke as he groaned and pulled the pillow over his head. Mondays were not his favorite days, and coming down to earth after yesterday's excitement wasn't going to be easy.

But this Monday started out just fine, with slaps on the back and congratulations from his classmates. He'd have preferred anonymity, but at least these were people he'd known all his life, not faceless reporters.

Then the day took off downhill.

In history class Mr. Shivan chose Jack to lead off the midterm oral reports the next day, and Jack was nowhere near ready. He was usually pretty well prepared for these things, but this one time he'd just put it off too long. With the weeklong buildup to the soccer matches, there was no way Jack could have settled down to work on a history report. Anyway, with twenty-six kids in the class, the odds were that he wouldn't have to give his report until Thursday or Friday. But now he faced a long, grueling night of research.

And then he discovered that he hadn't closed his water bottle tightly enough that morning, so the leftover slices of pesto pizza in his lunch bag had turned into dripping green mush.

On the other hand, Mary's Monday moved along much more smoothly.

After her pizza lunch—one slice—she went out to run a mile around the school track. She was pushing herself, getting ready for a meet, and this was one of those days when she felt like the wind. Just over seven minutes later, she hit the finish line and staggered to a

3

stop on the grassy field inside the track. Pulling out a dog-eared notebook from her backpack, which she'd put there beforehand, she flipped quickly to the page marked "Training" and sat down.

"Just call me *Acinonyx jabatus,*" she murmured as she noted her time. Mary's favorite subject was biology, and she delighted in the scientific names of animals.

"I thought your name was Mary." Her head jerked up toward the voice. "Or is it Cheetah Mary?" Allan Grant stood against the sun, grinning at her embarrassment.

Allan was an exchange student from Scotland, and he sat behind Mary in math. He was apparently pretty good at biology, too. He glanced at her notebook entries and let out a slow whistle of admiration. "Trying out for the Olympics, are you?"

Mary snatched the book and stuffed it into her backpack. "Nope. Just trying to increase my distance and speed."

"I like to run, too. Perhaps we can train together sometime. Do you fancy Friday?"

"Sure," she said. "But I don't usually run against boys."

"Don't worry about it," Allan said. "You won't beat me by too much, Cheetah Mary. Bye."

Mary watched him amble to the edge of the bleachers, where he looked back and waved to her. She sighed and looked dreamily up at the fluffy white clouds floating above. But just for a moment, before she shook her head impatiently and said to herself, "Earth to Mary! Come in please!" After all, Jack was the dreamer; she was the realist.

4

*   *   *

"Hey! How's my super soccer-playing bro?" Mary called to Jack cheerfully as he passed her by on their way home from school that afternoon. He just scowled at her and kept walking.

She caught up with him. "Jack! Wait up! You look like a *Bradypus tridactylus* with ingrown toenails."

Despite his best efforts, that got his attention. "A Brady what?" he asked.

"A three-toed sloth, of course!" Unfortunately for Jack, who was well into his suffering, it was almost impossible to be depressed when Mary was happy, and that was most of the time.

The Chamness twins squabbled only occasionally (they *were* human, and worse, they *were* brother and sister). Always, however, they looked out for one another. When Jack mentioned the pizza fiasco, Mary immediately produced an apple-cinnamon granola bar from her stash of healthy snacks.

As they walked home, Jack talked about his dismal day and bemoaned the grim evening he would have to spend with his nose in the encyclopedia. Mary, though not taking history this semester, had heard about what a demanding teacher Mr. Shivan was, so she knew there was no way to fake a report. Then she had a thought.

"Weren't the new museum acquisitions supposed to arrive today?" The days when the twins were able to preview new items in their father's museum were always fun. Despite their differences, both had inherited a love of history from their father—and if there were something in the mix Jack could take off on, his report might not be such a trial after all.

They hurried on. Bill Chamness was just pulling into the museum parking lot as the kids arrived, and he waved to them, flashing a big smile.

"I've just picked up something really special for the medieval exhibit," he announced, wiggling his eyebrows mysteriously as he dangled a tiny package in front of their surprised faces. "Come inside and take a look." Jack and Mary had hoped for a carload of treasures, but they followed the bait into the museum.

Two

"A TINY LITTLE BOOK?"

They were sitting in the living room of their apartment in the museum. Mary's kitten, Scuba, had jumped into her lap and was purring contentedly as she stroked the soft calico fur. Jack's question came out as more of a growl.

Their dad was examining the book, oblivious, as the twins looked at each other. Books were not a likely source of research-paper material, unless they were Gutenberg bibles or the first edition of the Federalist Papers. "That's nice, Dad," Jack said in a more normal tone—a carefully neutral tone. He'd have to get out of there and get going on his own research as soon as possible.

But Mary bent forward to take a closer look at the book. It measured a scant 3½ inches by 2½ inches and was, definitely, a tiny masterpiece, with skillfully illustrated and calligraphed parchment pages. The ornate Gothic lettering especially fascinated her. "It's beautiful, Dad," she said, and was pleased to see him smile at her interest. "Where did you find it?"

"Le Musée des Antiquités in Carcassonne, France, has agreed to loan it to us for our exhibit on the Middle Ages. It's called a Book of Hours—a prayer book—and it was owned by a rich merchant's wife in the early fourteenth century. It was called a Book of Hours because the day was divided into eight sections by the church, and each time one of those special hours was struck on the church bells, the book's owner would recite an appropriate prayer."

"A prayer book?" Jack was puzzled. "Then why are there funny drawings in the margins? Here's one that looks like a monster."

"They do seem out of place, don't they? Actually it was quite common for an imaginative artist to have a little fun with the side illustrations. It was accepted as part of the job."

"A sacred book with monsters thrown in?" Jack was having a hard time with that one.

"People were just as inconsistent then as they are now. Why do *we* condemn violence and demand guns? Somehow this—the book—made perfect sense at the time. But here's the main reason I wanted this *particular* Book of Hours." Bill Chamness turned to the final page of the book and pointed to a short list of names. "The calligraphy was done by your very own ancestor, Philippe Fouché."

"Fouché—? He's the one who made the family tree, isn't he?" asked Mary.

"Exactly," answered their dad.

The family tree was the family treasure: a large, carefully preserved book with records of their family history extending far into the past. The ancestors of these present-day Chamnesses had started keeping records of births, deaths, and marriages in the fourth century A.D., a time when only royal houses were accustomed to doing so, because of an unusual and distinctive family trait: nearly every generation boasted at least one set of twins. Philippe Fouché, a master calligrapher (and father of twins himself), had filled a little over half of a massive volume with a careful compilation of family records in his own time, leaving space to be filled by later generations. And every hundred years or so since, the head of one branch of the family or another had hired a calligrapher of his time to bring the book up to date. Bill Chamness, the museum curator, was the logical owner of the book in this generation, and so it resided in a place of honor on a beautifully carved wooden pedestal in one corner of the room.

Having riffled through the family tree on several occasions, and now admiring the tiny Book of Hours, Mary found herself quite impressed with the talent of this great-great-great-something-something-grandfather.

She and her father walked over to the large volume, Jack following despite himself. Their dad very carefully opened the heirloom to a page near the middle. "See— here's Philippe, his wife Isabelle, and their twin children, Jacques and Marie, born in the year 1300 in Carcassonne, France."

"Jacques and Marie?" laughed Mary delightedly. "Shows how unimaginative you and Mom are, Dad!"

"Actually a lot of the twins have had some variation

9

on those names," her dad responded. "It's tradition. My sisters. Jacqueline and Marian—"

"I thought only monks did this kind of lettering work," Jack interrupted, beginning to see a history report in this after all. "Philippe Fouché wasn't a monk, if he had a wife and twin kids."

"No, no," laughed their dad. "By the twelfth century, there were quite a few other scribes writing out books for the wealthy. A rich man could commission a book on hunting or order one with romantic poetry to impress his wife. The calligrapher would work with an illuminator, who added colored decoration and gold or silver highlights. Then a bookbinder would put it all together."

Jack perked up even more. "Those are the guilds we learned about in history. Specialists in certain trades got together, kind of like unions today."

"Exactly!" said his dad. "The secrets of the craft were protected by the guild and passed on to the apprentices and the journeymen, the next level up, before they became masters. The guilds regulated the work of their members, ensuring a certain quality and setting the going rate for a product. They also helped out members' families in case of sickness or death."

Mary was still admiring the Book of Hours. "Boy, this is just the kind of job I would have loved if I'd lived back then. But I suppose only men got to do *real* work," she sighed.

"Oh, no. Wives and daughters often got involved in the family business."

After another ten minutes of detailing tiny treasures in the book, Mr. Chamness had to go check on the plans

10

for its exhibition, but he left the book with the twins, knowing he could trust them to be careful.

Mary was now studying the calligraphy in the family tree and comparing it to the Book of Hours. Scuba the cat, having lost a lap, strolled out to the kitchen, hoping she might get lucky.

"Look at this, Jack," Mary said, indicating some tiny writing in the margin next to the entry of the family of Philippe Fouché. "I've never noticed this before. It looks like a poem, and its title is 'Jacques et Marie.' Let's see how good our French is."

"I've got to get to work, sis."

"Come on. You're the language expert."

"Yeah, right!" Jack laughed sarcastically. "But tonight I have to be a history expert."

"Good, because it's historical French."

"Mary—"

"Jack . . ."

"All right, all right."

Jack and Mary began to slowly recite the cryptic poem—slowly because some of the words were different from modern French. But they carried each other along. . . .

> *"En cest lignage a toz tens deus;*
> *Par toz siecles naissent gemeus . . ."*

And all at once they were surrounded by a sparkling cloud of silver light which faded to red, spiraled around and *clung* to them. "What's happening?" gasped Mary, but her voice was beaten back by the encircling light. She reached out to touch her brother, whose body

11

seemed to be *becoming* the light. Convulsively he grabbed her hand, and the light pulsed and grew and abruptly exploded in a burst bright enough to blind anyone there. But there was no one there—not any more.

The twins had vanished.

Three

To the twins, on the other hand, it was the living room that vanished. For a moment there was nothing around but the light. Then it faded, and their wide eyes grew accustomed to . . . gloom.

The living room was gone. They were standing in a dim, low-ceilinged room filled with parchment and vellum, goose quills, and pots of ink.

But more than that—"they" were not Jack and Mary. Staring at each other, they saw two other teenagers, dressed in medieval styles of clothing.

"Jack?" That's what Mary thought she said, but it came out more like "Jacques?" The boy before her, dressed in tights and a tunic of blue wool, stared back at her with wide eyes. "Marie?"

She nodded slowly, as if her head might fall off—since it might not even be her head. But it felt like her head, from the inside. Except that there was more in it. "Jacques . . . I know who I am, in our time, but I also feel like I belong here. I recognize this place. It's our home!"

13

"And do you know—you're speaking French? Perfect . . . medieval French?" The boy took both his hands and felt his way down his face. When he got to his chin, he looked the girl straight in the eyes—the no-longer green eyes. "Somehow we've gone back in time, and now . . . we're our ancestors! We're Jacques and Marie!"

She nodded. It sounded stranger than it seemed to her, just then. The poem did it! The words make perfect sense now:

"In this lineage there are always two;
In all the centuries twins are born . . ."

Marie looked down at her burgundy dress and twirled around, holding out the full skirt to admire the soft woven fabric. A lock of her long hair fell forward over her shoulder. "Fantastic! Blond curly hair! I always wondered what that would be like. Yours is still light brown, but you have blue eyes now!"

"So do you!"

The twins laughed excitedly as they looked at their new surroundings. What light there was entered the room from two small glassless windows and fell upon broad worktables. Atop one of the tables lay a knife, a pumice stone, and a piece of parchment. On the other table were several sheets full of beautiful Gothic calligraphy. A polished metal mirror revealed a reversed and slightly distorted reflection of the writing.

Jacques crossed the small room, his soft leather shoes padding quietly on the stone floor. He opened a drawer of a massive wooden chest and examined the finished

14

books inside. Above the chest was a long shelf that held a basket of goose quills, various other tools, and a box of exquisite little blocks of color.

"How are you coming with the parchment preparation, Jacques?" a deep voice asked. Descending the steep and twisting staircase in one corner of the room was a middle-aged man. The twins knew immediately that he was Philippe Fouché, father of Jacques and Marie, their ancestor—and proprietor of this scriptorium.

"It's . . . uh . . . going well . . . ah . . . Father." Jacques struggled with everything in that little speech. What did he know about parchment preparation—or what the real Jacques called his parents, for that matter? But then, relaxing, he heard himself add, "This is an especially fine skin with no holes or stains. I've nearly finished smoothing the surface." He stiffened with surprise and looked at his sister, who could hardly contain her excitement.

As Philippe examined his son's work, he nodded and smiled, the corners of his eyes crinkling with pleasure. "My boy, you are indeed a talented apprentice. A family trait, of course! Perhaps next year you will create your masterpiece and become a journeyman scribe."

He turned to Marie. "And, my dear daughter, have you found any errors in the manuscript I've copied?" Philippe affectionately put his arm around her shoulder.

"No, Father. All of the spelling is correct, and you've not left out any lines this time." Marie looked at Jacques as if to say, "See how easy it is!"

"Ho! You'll not let me forget my blunder of last week! Fortunately your keen eyes caught that one before

Sir Francis saw it. Otherwise he might think twice before hiring me to do the tournament certificates next week.''

Marie nodded happily, realizing for the first time that she could see clearly without glasses.

"Well, I'm off to visit some possible customers this afternoon. These small prayer books are becoming so popular, every fancy lady must have one—luckily for us!'' Philippe slipped a sample book into his pouch. "I'm hoping many of them will choose our studio over Louis's. You know I don't like to speak ill of anyone, but that man irks me! He's been trying to take away some of my steady accounts, even though his work is of an inferior quality. If he keeps at it I'll have to report him to the guild.'' His handsome face was set in a thoughtful frown as he walked toward the door.

"Will you be back for supper?'' asked Marie. "We have some of the mutton stew left, and I'll buy some bread later.''

"Delicious! You've been a fine cook since your mother's been away. Not that you weren't a wonder beforehand, too, of course! I forgot to tell you that I had a message from her this morning: Aunt Sophie is feeling much better now, and your mother will return in just a few days.''

Philippe grabbed his cap from its hook and pulled it over his curly gray hair. "When you've finished your duties, children, go to Henri's workshop and see how he's coming along with the illustrations for Madame Dupuis's book. The middle folio is especially critical, so be sure to check that one. Our contract states that it

16

will be completed by her birthday, and that's only ten days from now. The bookbinder needs at least a week.''

Bright sunshine streamed into the room as he opened the heavy wooden door. "And don't forget to close the shutters and lock up carefully. We don't want the burglar who stole Henri's supply of silver leaf in *here*!'' Philippe scowled at the memory as he stepped out into the street, then turned to give them each a lingering smile. "But I'm not worried; I have great faith in you.''

Once the door closed behind him, Jacques let himself plop heavily back against a table. "Whew! That was too weird!'' He waved a hand at the room. "But I've always wanted to visit France. And we've got free accommodations!''

Marie felt excited, too, but she couldn't help wondering about the details of their situation. "Yeah, but *why* are we here? How'd we *get* here? Where did the *real* Jacques and Marie go? And what about Mom and Dad? Won't they be worried about us?'' Finally: "I've got a date to go running on Friday.''

Jacques looked at her thoughtfully. "I've got a strong feeling that it's okay for us to be here—that we're *supposed* to be here. We fit in so well that not even our 'father' knows we're not his 'kids,' after all. So let's hope everything's okay with Jacques and Marie, and at home. What else can we do?''

"We can try to go home—maybe by reciting that poem again.''

"Not if we're *supposed* to be here.''

"We can try.''

"Later maybe. I want to see why we've come.''

"Well, that's what I asked you: Why *did* we come?''

17

"I have no idea, but I imagine we'll find that out, probably real soon."

Marie's mouth twisted in a comical grimace. "I hate laid-back brothers," she said. But she nodded. "Okay, okay—we *are* here. I guess I can wait to see what happens. But not *too* long; I want to be home by Friday."

"So let's finish our duties, Marie, then go to Henri's workshop and see how he's coming along with the illustrations for Madame Dupuis's book. You know where that is, don't you?"

"Yes, Jacques, I do."

While Jacques finished preparing the parchment, Marie went up the steep stairs to explore the rest of the house (though it wasn't really exploring, because everything seemed perfectly familiar, as if she'd lived there all her life). The second-floor "solar" was the sitting room, where the family ate and relaxed together around a warm hearth. Their meals were brought upstairs from the kitchen area, on the ground floor behind the workshop.

Fragrant bunches of fresh herbs hung from hooks above the window, through which could be seen the family's vegetable garden below. Stalks of straw, called rushes, covered the floor. "It's funny to have this on the floor instead of carpets," thought Marie, "but it makes perfect sense just to sweep them out along with the dirt every now and then."

Her eye was caught by a framed picture hanging on the wall. It was, according to a small plaque affixed beneath, a portrait of Philippe and Isabelle painted by Henri, on the occasion of their fifteenth wedding anniversary six months before. Philippe stood tall, a middle-

18

aged man who looked confident and happy. Isabelle's blond hair was pinned up and mostly hidden behind a lacy white veil, a gift, Marie knew, from Philippe. Her arm was linked with her husband's as she gazed at him with contentment and affection, and Marie smiled as she felt the love that this family shared.

Leaning in the corner next to the painting was a long stick, called a distaff, with a clump of sheep's wool attached to one end. The light tan wool had been combed out and loosely bundled on the end of the stick, ready to be twisted into thread. It was her mother's distaff, and Marie knew that every household in the town, rich and poor alike, had one. She reached up and fingered the soft wool. "Perhaps I'll do some mending later," she thought, and, strangely, found the idea enjoyable.

On the next level up, just as she knew it would be, was the sleeping area with straw mattresses and colorful feather quilts. Beyond that were the stairs leading to the top floor of the house, narrower and even steeper than the ones below. But Marie stopped at their base, knowing as well as she knew anything now that her "father" had forbidden her to climb those stairs to the room above—a room sealed off by a strong oaken door. The part of her that was Mary Chamness played briefly with the idea of going up there anyway—*Mary* hadn't been told not to do it—but the part that was Marie Fouché was a dutiful daughter. She stepped back, her lips pressed shut perplexedly. She knew she wouldn't disobey Philippe. But that didn't stop her from wondering what secret lay beyond those ten steep steps. . . .

Four

HALF AN HOUR LATER, WITH THE PARCHMENT SUCCESS-
fully smoothed, Jacques and Marie set out into the town
of Carcassonne. They were completely enthralled as
they wandered the narrow cobblestone lanes, winding
between the thatch-roofed oak-and-plaster houses huddled in the shelter of the town's stone walls. But since
they were supposed to be familiar with it all, they tried
not to gawk too much. That's why they almost got hit
with the rotten food.

"Look out, Marie!" shouted Jacques, dragging his
sister under the overhanging second story of the home
they were passing, just in time. They both glared at the
splatter of slop by her feet.

"I wish he'd throw his waste out in the morning like
everyone else," Marie muttered. "What a stink!" But
a nearby pig scurried to the garbage and gobbled it
down with appreciative snorts.

The sounds of a busy town filled their ears as the
twins turned into the main road. A journeyman blacksmith named Laurent was pounding away on his anvil,

and the clang of his hammer seemed to keep time with the church bells in the distance. The smell of smoke from his furnace mixed with the odor of wet leather hanging in the saddlemaker's yard next door.

Standing at the door of the smith's shop, dressed in a fine cape and bejeweled felt hat, was a splendid gentleman.

"I don't mind a nick or two adding to the character of my sword, but the large dent in the middle goes beyond character to caricature, and may well alter the sweep of my thrust." Sir Francis de Boudinel, a knight usually found on his nearby estates, withdrew the sword from its scabbard and presented it to the blacksmith. Sunlight glinted off the razor edge of the cold metal blade.

"Yes, I see," replied Laurent, examining the weapon with a critical eye. "You've been in a battle, Sir Francis."

"A minor skirmish only. Fortunately no wounds to my body, but as you can see, my opponent made quite a mark on my weapon," said the knight. "I hope you will have it ready for the tournament next week."

"Certainly. Send your squire to retrieve it three days from now," answered Laurent. "I'll set it up as good as ever it was."

The twins stood and unabashedly watched Sir Francis as he left the shop and strolled up the road.

"A real knight!" Marie murmured to her brother. "This is so *cool*!"

Jacques grinned at her. "I'd rather see him in a full suit of armor with a white horse, but I guess he'll do."

Just then a wizened little man, his shoulders bent in

21

a permanent stoop, came running out of the local tavern. "Sir Francis! Sir Francis!" he called in a piping voice.

The knight came to an unwilling halt and answered with more than a touch of impatience. "Yes, what is it?" The nobility weren't accustomed to doing business in the road.

The twins stayed back, watching from behind a hay wagon. "It's Louis, Father's competitor!" whispered Jacques. "That guy is so slimy!"

Louis gave Sir Francis a syrupy smile and chirped, "I understand that the Viscount Brazelle has asked you to arrange for the award certificates to be presented at the tournament."

"That's right, but what has this to do with you?" asked Sir Francis.

"I am a scribe," said Louis, "and my studio creates the most beautiful certificates in Carcassonne. I would like to do this work for you."

Jacques and Marie exchanged a wary glance.

"Thank you, but I am quite satisfied with the work of Philippe Fouché. He has done some fine commissions for me in the past," said the knight.

"But, sir, I will not charge you as much, so perhaps your budget will allow you to also obtain a small gift for your wife," persisted the scribe.

Sir Francis gave him a hard look. "You are not trying to bribe me, are you?" he said angrily. "Because if you are, I'll haul you to the sheriff myself!"

"Oh, no! I would never do that!" gasped Louis. "I merely wished to—"

"Good day!" interrupted Sir Francis, stomping away.

Louis looked around quickly to see if anyone had

22

witnessed his embarrassment. He spied the tops of the twins' heads above the hay wagon and glared ferociously at them.

Laughing delightedly, Jacques and Marie spun around and hurried off in the opposite direction.

"Ha! I can't wait to tell Father about this," squealed Marie.

"Strikeout for Louis," answered Jacques. But something—not something he knew as Jacques, but something he knew as Jack on the soccer field with opponents coming from all angles—caused him to turn and look behind them. He saw Louis still watching them, with an expression of quizzical curiosity on his prematurely wrinkled face. The man made no move to follow them, however.

So Jacques turned his attention back to the town around them, and all its modes of activity. Beautiful colors were blowing on the afternoon breeze as they made their way down a street of open-fronted shops; in honor of the upcoming tournament, the merchants had hung celebratory banners from nearly every rooftop.

Glancing into the alleyway between the shoemaker and the wool shop, Marie stopped short. "There's an unlikely duo," she thought as she watched a disheveled old man gesturing at a slim, well-dressed gentleman. The former was the hermit Renard, who lived in the forest well outside town, appearing only when he had something to buy or sell at the market. Today, judging by the bundled load at his feet, he was selling wood, but with the forest all around them, he wouldn't get much for that.

The other man reached into the sleeve of his dark blue

23

velvet mantle and handed something to Renard. Their transaction was mumbled, but Marie caught the words ". . . within the hour. . . ." The gentleman's back was turned, but a slight shift of his head enabled her to see his neatly trimmed black beard. "Could that be Monsieur Dupuis?" she wondered, thinking about the man whose wife had ordered the prayer book from her father.

Then, shaking her head impatiently, she chided herself, "Don't be so nosy, Marie! This is none of your business!" And she hurried up the lane to catch up with her brother, who had been lured by the heavenly aroma of roasting almonds.

After Jacques bought a bag for the two of them, using small coins he found in a leather pouch on his belt, they continued their stroll, munching hungrily. They found shade under the ancient sycamores that ringed the market. A trio of acrobats was tumbling among the trees.

In honor of business as usual, the merchants there were extolling the virtues of their wares. "Wool cloth for a new gown, mademoiselle? Ah, this sky blue one matches your lovely eyes."

"Some cheese for you, mademoiselle? The finest chèvre from healthy goats!"

"Sausage?"

"Fruit?"

Then, through all the noise, came the exquisite sound of a mandolin and one clear voice, singing the *Song of Roland:*

> *"The lord have mercy on thy soul*
> *Never more shall our fair France behold*
> *A knight so worthy, till France be no more."*

"A troubadour!" Marie grabbed her brother's arm and pulled him closer to the small crowd surrounding the young man. He was very handsome, with raven locks that fell to the center of his shoulder blades.

An elderly woman with tears in her eyes dropped a coin into the open hat on the ground next to the singer. "That sad story always makes me bawl. Always. You have a strong voice, lad . . . yet your accent is not French. Where do you come from?"

"From Italy, madame. A small town in the north." He smiled at the woman. "I thank you for your kind donation."

The boy appeared to be about eighteen, and his dark eyes glanced at them in a friendly way, bringing a blush to Marie's cheeks.

"We need to be going, Marie," said her brother as he gave her a gentle tug, "or we'll never finish our errands before supper."

Marie sighed as she reluctantly followed Jacques. Brothers had no souls. But just then a pretty girl around their own age, wearing a white bonnet over her dark hair, appeared in front of them as if by magic. "Oh, good afternoon, Marie. How are you? Is your mother back yet?" But before Marie could answer her, the girl turned her gaze exclusively on Jacques. "Hello to you, too, Jacques. I've been considering what you asked me yesterday, and I think I'd like it very much. We should discuss it . . . perhaps Thursday? I have the afternoon off."

"Well . . . uh . . . Thursday's fine . . . ah . . . Josiane," Jacques stammered, reddening. He knew she was Jacques's girlfriend, and in this day and age, people could get married when they were thirteen. He knew Jacques had asked her to go swimming in the moonlight this weekend. Now *he* was Jacques, and he (Jack) had never seen her before in his life.

Marie came to the rescue. "Josiane! No, Mother's not back yet. Our aunt Sophie is feeling much better, but you know how nasty those colds can be, at her age especially. Mother does hope to be back for the tournament next week. Sorry we can't talk now, but we're just on our way to Henri's to check some manuscripts."

Jacques picked up the ball. "Sure, Josiane, Thursday should be . . . fine. I'll pick you up at the bakery when you finish work. Two o'clock?"

Josiane nodded happily and with a wave she was gone.

Jacques looked at Marie appreciatively. "Thanks, sis. I'm glad you're on my team."

"Just don't give me a hard time about the troubadour," she said with eyebrows arching, and started off down the road.

Soon they came to the Dupuis glass shop. Beautiful vases and bowls were displayed on the shelves within, and the merchant was showing an exquisite glass tray to a customer.

"There's Monsieur Dupuis," said Marie, noticing his dark blue cape. "I *thought* I saw him with Renard behind the wool shop, not ten minutes ago. But I didn't see him go past us."

"Your eyes were glued to that singer! Oops, sorry." His sister elbowed him reflexively, but her mind was on the man in the shop.

"You will notice, Madame Cruard, how the artist so

26

skillfully applied the gold along the scalloped edges,'' said Monsieur Dupuis. Madame Cruard examined the work with a critical eye, but in the end nodded her satisfaction.

Marie wanted to stop here as well. ''I could spend hours just looking in these shops. It's fascinating; there's so much to see,'' she sighed.

''Duty calls,'' said Jacques, pulling her along. Now that his sister had stopped worrying about the details of their strange transformation, she was caught up in the details of their new existence. Why couldn't she just go with it, like he did? It was indeed fascinating, but he liked to drink it in as a whole, all the colors and smells and songs mixed together.

They walked past another two side streets, then up a narrow passageway, the pleasant fragrance of tarragon and thyme floating on a light breeze. Someone was going to eat well tonight.

Henri's studio was at the far end of the passage. As they approached it, they suddenly saw that the door was standing slightly ajar. The twins came to an uncertain halt. This couldn't be good; Henri would definitely have locked his door after the recent burglary, and double-checked it. Holding his breath, Jacques reached out, knocking lightly . . . and the heavy door swung slowly wide, creaking on its hinges.

In the time they came from, the twins would have thought long and hard about walking into a gloomy, unknown shop, but this time seemed too ''quaint'' to have any real dangers. So they stepped across the threshold, and learned a lesson: The shop had been completely ransacked! Chairs were overturned, drawers pulled out, and artist's materials strewn everywhere. A smear of something red marked the floor, but Marie was momentarily relieved to discover that it was only dirt.

Jacques, meanwhile, pushed past her toward a worktable. Something was pinned there with an evil-looking knife. Yanking the blade free, he lifted the piece of parchment and read: *"Do not seek your master or he will die! Be silent, and he shall return unharmed in two days' time."* The writing was messy, and ink had smudged the edge of the parchment where the writer had grasped it. Jacques handed the note to Marie for her perusal.

Just then a door in the back of the house slammed shut.

Five

MARIE JAMMED THE NOTE INTO HER POCKET AS THE TWINS stumbled across the room into the kitchen. They reached the narrow alley behind the studio just in time to catch a glimpse of a red-capped figure disappearing around a corner.

"Quick!" shouted Jacques. "We can't let him get away!"

Marie raced after him. "No matter how pretty these clothes are, I sure do miss my jeans and sneakers right now," she thought as she tripped awkwardly in the long skirt. But even with impediments, she was the fastest of the three.

Into the main road they ran, dodging peddlers and chickens, both squawking, as they strained to keep an eye on their quarry.

"Watch out, Jacques!" screamed Marie as a fast-moving horse and cart squealed around a corner, barely missing the boy.

"Hey, where did you get your driver's license?" Jacques yelled. The man holding the reins gave him a look adults have given teenagers since long before the fourteenth century, but kept on moving.

In the time it took to avoid getting run over, the twins had lost sight of the fugitive. They looked frantically around, trying to spot the red cap again, and were dismayed to see five of them.

"There aren't a lot of fashion statements in medieval times," snapped Jacques.

"There! That one's running!" Marie pointed to a figure just dissolving into a crowd at the market square, a block down the street.

"I see him!" yelled Jacques. "See if you can cut him off by running around the square. I'll go this way." He plunged into the throng of people as Marie took off to the right. She knew that although she had the speed, he was best at maneuvering through traffic. But in the end, it was she who got around the crowd in time to block the way of a frightened red-capped boy carrying a soccer ball—a boy she knew.

"François!" No longer bothering to think "I know this but I didn't used to," Marie recognized the eleven-year-old apprentice of Henri the illuminator. His freckled face had turned pink with the exertion of running, and his damp red hair was plastered to his forehead; he looked like a winded tomato.

Jacques dashed out of the marketplace and gaped at the boy. "François! Why in the world did you run from us?"

All three of them were trying to catch their breath. As one, they moved away from the crowd. "I didn't know it was you!" gasped François, looking up at his older friends. "I was scared. Someone has kidnapped Henri!"

"So we gathered," said Jacques. "What do you know about it?"

François looked embarrassed. "Nothing, I'm afraid. I—I had just gotten back to the workshop; I'd been on an errand to the parchmenter. I was supposed to get back earlier, but I stopped to play a little soccer." He added hopefully, "*You* know, Jacques . . ."

"That's right," said Marie, nodding. "My bro's a super soccer star in any era."

"Bro?" asked François.

"Never mind," said Jacques firmly, giving his sister a warning look. "Keep going."

"Well, when I got back, Henri was gone, and the place was torn apart. Stuff was thrown everywhere. Then I saw a message that said someone had taken him." François's hand flew to his mouth. "Oh, no! I wasn't supposed to tell anyone!"

"It's okay, François, we saw the note, too," said Marie. "Do you have any idea who could have done it?"

"No, Marie—everybody liked Henri. I'm so afraid, I don't know what to do!" François looked ready to cry.

"Don't worry, we're going to figure this out." She turned to her brother. "Aren't we?"

"Sure we are. This may be the reason we're here."

"To be detectives?" Marie asked.

"Heck, *I* don't know. But we're certainly not going to ignore anything this interesting."

"*I'd* like to be home by Friday," she answered. But

31

that was just standard brother-baiting; she had to admit this was an exciting turn of events.

"I think it's best not to alert the sheriff yet," Jacques said. "We don't want to risk Henri getting killed." He looked around, but nobody seemed to be paying any attention to them; they were just three kids with a soccer ball. "I admit, I wish I knew where Father was right now, but I guess we can handle this."

"Was anything missing from the workshop, François?" asked Marie.

"Yes. I noticed right away, someone took all of the pages from the Book of Hours Henri and your father were crafting for Madame Dupuis. Except for these pages, that is." The eleven-year-old pulled a small parchment folio from the sleeve of his tunic. There were two completed pages of the book on one side and two more on the reverse.

François handed the folio to the twins. "I took this piece to the parchmenter to see if he had another sheepskin of this fine quality. Henri wanted to match it for another project he's doing."

Jacques and Marie examined the pages carefully and then exchanged a knowing glance. These were the very pages they had seen as Jack and Mary almost seven centuries later, only the colors were far brighter because they'd just been made.

"These illustrations in the borders are very strange," said Jacques, pointing out a gargoyle and a seven-pointed star. Maybe now he could get a better explanation than his real father's "They just did that."

"And look at this on the other side," added Marie. "A three-legged dog. What does *it* mean?"

32

François shrugged and shook his head. "I don't know. Henri and Philippe were talking about the illustrations last week when I came into the room, but they stopped talking when they saw me, so it must have been a secret."

"A secret that might hold the answers we need to find Henri," mused Jacques. "And we know that somebody wants these pages, so we've got to make darn sure that somebody doesn't get them." He looked down at the ball François was carrying. It was homemade, and not particularly round, with scraps of parchment over wadded felt, sewn together with bookbinders' heavy thread. One strand was coming loose, and Jacques gave it a little tug, unraveling it more.

Looking around to again make certain that no one was watching them, Jacques tucked the 3½-inch book pages into the stuffing of the soccer ball. He quickly restrung the thread and knotted it, securing the pages inside.

"Marie, go to Madame Dupuis's home and see what she can tell you about the illustrations for her book," said Jacques. "I'll roam around and see if I can track down the three-legged dog or any of the other clues. François, someone may well be looking for you, since you're Henri's apprentice, so take the soccer ball and hide with it in the church. You'll be safe there. I'll come for you in two hours—an hour before sundown. Marie, we'll meet you back at Father's scriptorium. Synchronize your watches."

"Synchronize your what?" François asked.

"Uh, never mind. Just another expression," muttered Jacques. Now it was Marie's turn to give her brother a warning look. Then the three hurried off in different directions.

Six

Marie briskly strode along the main street toward
the home of the Dupuis family, who lived on the far
side of town.

As she walked she thought about the miracle that had
brought her and her twin brother to this medieval French
town. "This sure is different from my peaceful life back
home," she mused. "The most I ever had to worry
about was having a bad-hair day or getting homework
done. Today I'm trying to find a kidnapper who has
threatened to kill my father's friend!"

She looked back over her shoulder toward the crowd
at the market square, and her eyes settled for a moment on a tall figure dressed in a hooded black cloak.
"He must be burning up in that cloak. Like an *Ovis
aries* who missed his wool-shearing appointment," she
chuckled.

"Hey! Watch where you're going, mam'selle!"
Marie nearly collided with an old man stooped under a
heavy burden of firewood. It was Renard, the hermit
from the forest.

"I'm so sorry, I wasn't paying attention," Marie said as she stepped around the man. She leaned over and picked up a leather pouch that had fallen from its place between two thick sticks. A slender thong was laced around the bag to keep it tightly closed, but Marie could feel the corners of several solid items inside.

"Give me that!" the old man said harshly, glaring at the girl. One eye was clouded over with a whitish cornea; the pupil of the other was so dilated that the iris appeared black. Marie shivered with the feeling that the hermit was able to look directly into her soul, and see what a fraud she was. She quickly placed the bag upon the load of wood, then watched as the man lurched away.

She was puzzled by his rudeness when she was only trying to help, but shook it off. "Maybe *he's* just having a bad-hair day. Anyway, I've got too many problems of my own to worry about him."

She walked a little farther past some shops and cafés before entering the neighborhood of the Château Comtal. This was the property of the Viscount Brazelle, who had ordered the award certificates for the tournament. Most of the wealthy families lived in this part of town, clustered around the castle in spacious stone houses with beautiful gardens.

Playing in the shade of a sycamore tree were two well-dressed little girls and their frisky gray kitten. Their young nanny, hardly older than Marie, was sitting nearby, and a picnic of fruit and cheese was spread out on the grass beside them. When the cat spied another girl, he romped over to Marie and arched his back for appreciation.

"Oh, what a pretty kitty!" Marie knelt down to stroke the playful ball of fur. "My kitty at home is calico."

"What's her name?" asked one of the girls, wandering over.

"Scuba," answered Marie. "We found her one day on the beach after we'd gone . . ." She was about to say scuba diving but caught herself just in time. "Just after we'd gone wading in the water."

"That doesn't follow," said the older girl officiously, but her sister just giggled.

"Scuba's a funny name. Our kitty is named Thistle, because he has prickly claws and we found him in the thistle plants," said the younger girl. "And *my* name is Whistle . . . so Thistle and Whistle! And *her* name," she said, giggling harder as she pointed at her big sister, "is Gooba . . . so Gooba and Scuba!"

"It is not, you dummy!" the other girl yelled indignantly. She began to chase her sister around the sycamore tree. "Your name is Doodoo, but mine is Aurelie . . . Aurelie de Boudinel!"

"Girls! Stop this now! Or this young lady will think you are naughty rascals!" said the nanny, clapping her hands to get their attention. She turned to Marie. "You've been to the sea! I've never met anyone who's been there."

"Ah, well, only once, and not for very long," mumbled Marie. She was big on biology but not geography; how far from the sea was Carcassonne? Quickly changing the subject, she asked, "Can you direct me to the home of the Dupuis family?"

"Certainly. Just turn right at the large house there," the young woman said, nodding toward an ancient stone building. "Head away from the castle, and go to the end of the road. You'll see some lilac bushes near the door. Pull the bell and the servant will answer."

Marie thanked her and stepped back into the street, first checking both ways for fast-moving carts. She was startled to see the black-cloaked man ducking quickly into the candle shop back down the road.

"He's following me!" thought Marie. "Well, I'll give him a run for his money!" She strolled slowly toward the large house, then turned left, and as soon as she was out of sight, she ran flat out down the narrow road toward the castle. This time she held her skirts in one hand, freeing her legs. Tall buildings cast long shadows over the winding lane, and Marie's eyes were sweeping them for a hiding place.

Finally she saw what she wanted: a narrow passage between two houses. Ducking in, she hid, catching her breath. "I'll wait until he passes, and then I'll follow *him*. Maybe he'll lead me to Henri."

A few seconds later, her straining ears picked up the sounds of hurrying footsteps on the cobblestones. Closer and closer they came, and she pressed herself more tightly into her small niche, hardly daring to breathe at all. Her heart was racing as she glimpsed the black cloak brushing past her, inches from the passage entrance.

One thought hammered in her brain: "Don't look this way . . . please don't look this way!" And he didn't. Moving steadily, he passed by and was gone.

She slipped out of the secret nook, grateful for the obscuring shade, and began to follow at a safe distance as the mysterious man crept farther down the road. Now the tables were turned.

But suddenly the cloaked figure stopped. He tilted his head slightly, as if thinking something through. Then he began to turn around, slowly . . . slowly . . .

"Hey! You're going the wrong way!"

Marie spun instinctively, and saw Aurelie skipping energetically toward her.

"This is the way to my house! You can come visit if you want to!" the little girl said brightly as she grasped the teenager's hand.

Marie whipped her head back around to check on the man in the cloak, but he had melted away into the shadows.

Seven

"ORANGE, BOY?"

Jacques looked askance at the two filthy urchins who were holding up a sad and well-worn fruit, of a color closer to brown. "No, no orange," he said firmly. "I'm looking for a dog with just three legs. Have you seen one in this area?"

The boys exchanged a knowing glance. "Could be," said the taller one, cocking an eyebrow. "What's it worth to you?"

Jacques reached into his pouch and fished out a centime.

The boy turned the small coin over in his grimy hand and examined it carefully. "Nope. Not in *this* area," he replied, his mouth twisting into a smirk.

"Then where?" Jacques growled, putting on his most fearsome expression and clutching the front of the boy's torn tunic.

"One more centime!" the little rogue demanded, sticking out his chin.

Jacques had to laugh as he released the boy. "I like

your spirit," he said, reaching into his pouch for another coin.

Only when each child had his centime did they deign to continue. "We saw a dog like that yesterday, didn't we, Luc?" The child looked at his friend.

"Yes. It was gnawing a bone in front of the wineshop over by the west gate. I remember because it limped over to me when I dropped my sausage, gobbled it right up." Luc looked thoughtful. "It was one of the back legs that was missing. Right, Patric?"

"That's right." Patric gestured toward the distant city wall. "About six blocks in that direction. You know Old Gilbert's wineshop, don't you? That's where we saw the dog."

"I know Gilbert—my father sometimes shops there— but the dog was never around before. Thank you, boys. You're crafty little businessmen." Jacques smiled as he headed off down the road.

"Wait!" Patric yelled, and Jacques turned around just in time to catch the orange the boy tossed to him.

Jacques then continued on his way toward the west gate, determined to solve the puzzle of the manuscript illustrations. "Let's see . . . a dog I might be able to find. And I've seen gargoyles on the cathedral, and the jewelers' guildhall. They're drain spouts for rainwater, designed to look like monsters."

He savored his dried-out orange as he considered possibilities. "I wonder if Henri is being held captive in a building with gargoyles. Doesn't seem very likely, but the guildhall's not far from here. I could check that later." Jacques picked a piece of orange pulp from between his front teeth. "Still, how does that seven-pointed star fit in? Christians like five points, Jews six, but what can seven mean?''

His thoughts were interrupted by the sharp sting of a small pebble on the back of his neck. He looked around quickly to see Vincent, the young apprentice of Louis, his father's rival in the calligraphy business.

''Nyaa! Got you, you two-bit scribe!'' taunted Vincent, making a face and sticking out his tongue at the surprised Jacques.

Jacques made a lunge at the younger boy, who evaded his grasp and took off down a narrow passageway, howling with laughter.

''You little creep!'' shouted Jacques. ''Get a life! I don't have time for your stupid games!'' He waved his fist at the kid, then turned and hurried on his way . . . remembering ruefully that it wasn't that long since he'd been a kid himself. But was he ever that . . . annoying? Maybe it wasn't a question that wanted an answer.

The neighborhood he came to seemed full of activity, with dogs barking and children squealing as they played a game of tag. A couple of washerwomen were gossiping as they hung out their laundry on frayed ropes, and two hard-of-hearing old men belabored each other about ''the good old days.''

Jacques found he had to chuckle. ''Things really weren't any different back in this time, at all,'' he thought, tucking his leftover orange-half into his pouch.

But two blocks farther, things quieted significantly. Though there were still people to be seen, no one was talking. Many of the wealthy merchants had their businesses in the area of the west gate, and Jacques knew that this part of town was usually very lively. But the people just sat or strolled as if each was alone in his own private world.

For some reason a chill ran up Jacques's back. He turned to look back the way he'd come. Yes, there were still children playing there; the normal world still rolled on. But was the sunlight just a little brighter there?

A well-dressed man brushed past him without a word or a glance. Jacques recognized him as the importer of fine jewelry. A brooch with a seven-pointed star was pinned to his cloak.

"Monsieur Pradet!" called Jacques. But the man just gave him a cursory nod and kept walking.

Jacques felt a strong attraction for walking right behind him, keeping on until he got back to the neighborhood of cheerful people. But there was nothing overtly threatening about the people here; after all, they were ignoring him. And what would he tell Marie if he chickened out now? He was the one who'd given her and François their orders, and handed this job to himself. He was the one who'd figured he and his sister had come back in time for a reason.

But he did allow himself to wish he had a team alongside him now. "All right, then; just head on to Old Gilbert's wineshop," he thought.

The boy stepped into the musty store and looked around in the gray light for the old man. The aroma of fermented grapes had settled heavily throughout the room, and the walls were lined with large wooden barrels filled with wine. Gilbert was extremely fond of his product, and the wine always seemed to energize him. Jacques had never seen him when he wasn't talking away a mile a minute. But now there was no sign of human habitation.

"Gilbert, are you here?" Jacques called. He moved farther into the dim space, circling the barrels and nearing the cellar where the finest wines were kept. The trapdoor yawned upward on its rope hinges, revealing a dark square in the floor. The rope ladder that usually led downward had been pulled up and left to sprawl haphazardly beside the opening. "Gilbert?"

Suddenly a shove from behind sent him crashing into the pit. For a sickening moment there was nothing but blackness and empty space—then his flailing arms hit damp dirt, hard, protecting his face but wrenching his left wrist and shoulder.

"Vile creature! Son of the evil wizard!" screamed a voice above him.

Jacques scrambled to his feet, massaging his aching wrist. He looked up to the square of dim, dusty light five feet above his head and saw the silhouettes of a thin, stooped man and a thinner dog, leaning down toward the hole. Was it the three-legged dog? Jacques couldn't see its back end.

"You're mistaken, Gilbert!" yelled the boy. "My father's a good man!"

As his eyes became accustomed to the dark, Jacques spotted a seven-pointed star pinned to the old man's clothes. "What does that symbol mean?" he demanded. "And what's happened to Henri?"

Gilbert hissed back at the boy. "I'll answer no questions from you, you sprite of Hades! The hour of the miracle is near, and the crimson gargoyle abides no

43

unbelievers. In this pit you'll conjure nothing to foil the magic of the great Gurawl!''

He slammed the trapdoor closed and drove the wooden peg solidly through the latch. The sounds of the dog's low growl and the old man's cackle penetrated the heavy trapdoor, sending shivers down Jacques's spine.

Then all was silent.

Eight

"MADAME DUPUIS IS NAPPING NOW, MADEMOISELLE, BUT she should arise in a few minutes, if you'd care to wait."

Marie stood at the door of the great lady's house, nodding at the servant, Benjamin, who'd come in answer to her hail, but she quickly turned one last time to see if the cloaked man had reappeared behind her. As best as she could tell, he hadn't. "I'd be happy to wait," she replied.

"This way, mademoiselle," the man replied, ushering her into the sitting room of the elegant home. Marie knew most everyone in the town, at least by sight—she had seen Monsieur and Madame Dupuis riding in their carriage from time to time—but she had never in her life been inside such a glorious dwelling as this. There was not much more furniture than in her own home, but the benches and stools were beautifully made. Along one wall was a large mahogany chest, ornately carved. Above it hung a small, intricately embroidered tapestry, depicting a garden scene with playful animals and flowering trees.

Marie approached a wooden shelf that held several exquisite glass vases. "How lovely!" she exclaimed. "I've never seen any glasswork so fine."

"They are beautiful, aren't they?" said Benjamin, picking up a transparent pink vase with delicate petals attached around the rim. "Monsieur Dupuis found this one on his last trip to Italy. It is Venetian glass from the last century, and the pink color is caused by the addition of a certain chemical to the molten glass."

"And this one?" asked Marie, admiring a slim bottle. "How were the colored stripes made?"

"Ah, this ancient treasure is from Egypt, though I have seen similar ones in the eastern Mediterranean countries. The artist used a sand mold and wrapped thin rods of different colored glass around it. When cooled, the sand is removed and the striped glass remains."

"My glass collection is a great pleasure to me," said a soft, cultured voice from behind Marie. The girl turned to see a lovely woman, wearing a flowing veil and a light blue dress, entering the room. Madame Dupuis smiled at her young visitor. "I am fortunate, because my husband is an importer of fine glass, and he has given me many beautiful things," she said.

"Good afternoon, madame," said Marie with a curtsy. "My name is Marie Fouché. I am the daughter of Philippe Fouché, the scribe who is crafting the Book of Hours you commissioned."

"Yes, of course, you resemble him very much. There's no trouble with the book, is there?"

"Oh no, madame."

"Well then, would you like to have some cider with me in the garden?" With a gracious sweep of her arm, the lady invited Marie to walk with her down the short hallway. Though her manner remained friendly, the volume of her voice had risen, even though they were closer together now. "Perhaps," Marie thought, "she spoke softly at first to avoid startling me and making me drop the vase. As if I would!"

As they were about to enter the courtyard, Madame Dupuis picked up her distaff from its place by the door and began to idly twist the wool as she carried it outside with her.

"I would like to ask you some questions about the book, if you please," began Marie as she seated herself on a stone bench beside fragrant rosebushes. A vine of pink honeysuckle trailed along the beautifully constructed wall that bounded two sides of the garden, and humming bees drifted lazily in and out of the decorative opening in a narrow gate.

Madame Dupuis, sitting down across from the girl, said, "Certainly, Marie. What is it that you would like to know?"

"I know that your birthday is soon, but was there any other reason why you asked to have the book made at this time?" asked Marie.

The lady cocked her head and seemed to consider her visitor. "Yes, there was another reason," she began, but stopped again—gratefully?—as Benjamin arrived bearing the cider and some dainty cakes on a platter. Madame Dupuis put down her distaff as she accepted her cup and lost herself in its spicy aroma. Benjamin put the platter on a small table nearby and left them.

A silent moment passed.

Finally the lady began again. "The Book of Hours

47

will guide me in my daily prayers, and in these times of trial, prayer is our fervent hope. Because . . ." Madame Dupuis looked directly into Marie's questioning eyes at last, "because a rumor has been circulating amongst the women of the court of a strange, diabolical cult. I believe there is great evil afoot, and it terrifies me!"

"What sort of evil? Who's in the cult?" asked Marie, leaning forward excitedly.

"No one knows exactly. Some say the merchants control it, but my husband would know if *that* were true. He just scoffs and calls it gossip. Undoubtedly there is wicked magic involved. But those who believe in the true religion need never come to harm. That is my comfort, so I shall pray with all my heart." Madame Dupuis looked reverently to the heavens and gave a shuddering sigh. She looked so saintly that Marie was reluctant to interrupt her holy thoughts. But Henri was missing and there was little time for such etiquette.

"Have you seen the drawings in the margins of your book?" the girl asked.

The lady blinked, startled out of her reverie, and thought for a moment before responding. "Yes, your father showed me sketches to be approved."

"Do they have special significance?" inquired Marie. "There was a three-legged dog."

"No special meaning to me," answered the lady. "I know that Philippe and Henri like to add their personal touches, drawings of animals and other things. It's customary to allow the artists some freedom, and I accept that."

"What about the gargoyle and the seven-pointed star?"

"Philippe suggested that the gargoyle would scare away evil spirits. I like the star . . . perhaps it symbolizes hope?" Madame Dupuis smiled at the thought.

Marie finished her cider; there was nothing more to be learned here. She thanked Madame Dupuis for her hospitality. "I'm sure you'll be very pleased with your prayer book. My father has worked hard to make it special for you."

But the lady was still ruminating on current affairs. "Perhaps you should go to the castle and talk to my friend, Lady Chantal de Boudinel. She and her husband, Sir Francis, are guests of the viscount this month, and she hears a lot of talk around the court. She is the one who has told me most about the cult."

"Oh, I don't think I could go to the *castle,*" said the daughter of a guildsman.

Madame Dupuis laughed for the first time. "Don't worry, Marie. Lady Chantal loves to talk . . . and the more people she talks to, the more people she can talk about. Just tell her I sent you."

"Well . . . thank you, madame. I'll do that."

Madame Dupuis rang a small glass bell near at hand, summoning Benjamin to escort Marie to the door. Once they were out of earshot, he said, "I'll be off in a few minutes to do the shopping for tonight's supper. Would you like a ride somewhere in the cart?"

"You are very kind, but I enjoy walking in the late afternoon." Idle conversation, another's cart: these would only slow her down.

Suddenly Monsieur Dupuis came rushing through the

door, carrying a small bundle wrapped in silken cloth. He looked startled when he saw Marie, and clutched his package close to his chest.

"Oh! For a moment I thought you were my wife," he said. "Excuse me, but I am in a hurry."

Marie moved to the side as the man dashed past her and disappeared down the hallway. With a farewell nod to Benjamin, the girl stepped into the road and began to walk away. She listened for the click of the door's latch and the retreating footsteps of the servant before she quickened her pace, following the stone wall around the side of the property to the back gate.

"Darn! It's locked!" She groaned in frustration as she jiggled the handle. "Something's up with Monsieur Dupuis," she thought as she peered through the honeysuckle draped over the opening.

As if in answer, Monsieur Dupuis stepped out of the house and into the courtyard. His eyes darted here and there, and he quickly glanced over his shoulder as if to ensure that he was alone. Marie stood frozen outside the gate and silently exhaled in relief when he didn't spot her.

He walked directly to the rosebush beside the stone bench where Marie had sat, and squatted down behind it. With rapid movements he clawed at the ground, placed a small item into the hole, then firmly patted the loose dirt over it. He closed his eyes and mumbled a few words, which Marie's straining ears couldn't hear.

She watched him return to the house, her mind racing frantically. "I've got to get in and find out what he buried!" She reached through the aperture in the gate, but her stretched fingers were still inches away from the interior latch.

Looking up at the eight-foot wall, she determined to scale it, regardless of the jagged rocks on the top. "I'll just pad them with my skirt. This outfit should be good for something," she thought wryly.

But just as she found her first foothold in the stones that made up the wall, Marie heard laughter coming from the garden. Monsieur Dupuis was returning, now with Madame Dupuis. They seemed to be coming out for a stroll, and they were holding hands. Marie could have screamed in frustration; she was right on the verge of something, but her investigation would have to wait.

Nine

"OKAY, NOW. DON'T PANIC. 'COOL UNDER PRESSURE'—that's what they say about me," Jacques muttered as he stared up toward the blackness of the trapdoor. A thin line of pale gray light was visible around the edges, broken only by the latch on one side and the rope hinges on the other.

He moved gingerly around the tiny space, feeling his way carefully. By standing with his arms spread out, he could practically touch the boxes full of wine jugs stacked against the opposing damp earth walls at the same time.

Squeak! Something brushed Jacques's right foot, and he leapt hastily to the side.

"Gack! Rats!" The boy shivered as he heard the little bodies scuttering into a corner. "This place is *not* recommended in the guidebooks!"

Jacques raised his arms toward the trapdoor on the ceiling, but could only touch it by jumping as high as he could. The simple tap made his twisted wrist throb, and dusty cobwebs dangling from the edges of the door clung gently to his face.

52

He rubbed his wrist and wished his eyes would grow more accustomed to the dark, but it seemed they were as accustomed as they were going to get. "At least my wrist's just strained, not broken," he thought, carefully rotating the joint to test that proposition. "I'm going to need it, whatever I do here."

Jacques began cautiously inching his way to one side, occasionally swinging out a foot to ward off curious rats. His outstretched fingers again brushed the dusty top of a stack of wooden crates.

"This'll do," he thought as he lifted the top crate from the pile. The clay vessels inside clunked against each other as the crate shifted. He placed the box directly below the latch of the trapdoor, and stepped up on it. He pulled his penknife from his pouch and poked through the crack at the wooden peg.

"*Arghh . . .* this'll take about a million years! But . . ." The boy pushed up on the wooden square, which jiggled slightly at the hinged side. He stepped down and moved the crate a couple of feet over, and then tried again.

This time his penknife worked well against the worn rope of the hinges. In a short time, he had cut through and was able to push the trapdoor open with a loud bang.

Grrrr . . . Rrrrrr! The dog, now visible once more in the shop light, appeared at the side of the opening, baring his sharp teeth at Jacques. There was no sign of Gilbert in the shop; he had left the animal to guard his prisoner. The prisoner thought it had been an excellent decision, because foamy drool dripped from the dog's mouth.

53

"Could he be rabid?" Jacques wondered furiously. "They sure as heck didn't have a vaccine for that in the Middle Ages. Now what?"

Squeeeak!

Looking down past his crate, he spotted the rats staring back at him with beady red eyes. "Yeah!" Jacques muttered. "If Fido wants to bite something, I've got just the thing!" Quickly he stooped and reached for the black bundle of fur, which squeezed farther into its corner, hissing at him. But at the last moment, his brain caught up to his hand.

"A bite from a rabid rat would be just as bad as one from a dog! But how else can I . . . ?" And then he remembered his leftover orange.

With swift, sure movements, he retrieved the bit of fruit from his pouch. It was as dried out as ever, but he dangled it temptingly before dropping it a foot in front of the rat. The creature's tiny eyes followed it all the way to the ground, and it hesitated only briefly before scurrying over to the food, sniffing it and munching it hungrily.

Then Jacques pulled a clay jug from his crate and smashed the rat.

In an instant he had a hold on the long tail and flung the creature up and into a corner of the wineshop. It landed with a loud thud, and the dog lurched frantically away to investigate.

Wasting no time at all, Jacques hoisted himself out of the pit. The dog was intent on its tiny prey and didn't even glance at the boy, who raced out of the store and down the road. But Jacques was no longer concerned

54

with the dangers of the wineshop; he knew he'd only won round one.

"*Something's* going to be happening real soon . . . '*a miracle,*' Gilbert said. That must mean it's happening around here," thought Jacques, "since Gilbert was just leaving his shop—which makes the jewelers' guildhall, with its stone gargoyle, a likely place to look after all."

He hurried down an alley that led to the narrow lane running in front of the guildhall, but kept himself well hidden in the shadows in case Gilbert was anywhere around. Spotting the sheriff of Carcassonne strolling slowly in the lane, Jacques felt both relief and indecision. "I wonder if it would be best for me to ask for his help," he thought, biting his lip, "even though we were warned not to."

He had just decided to call a greeting to the sheriff, who hadn't yet seen him, when he noticed something pinned to the man's cloak. It was a seven-pointed star, shining cheerfully in the afternoon sunlight! Jacques felt as if he'd been kicked in the stomach.

Perhaps the sheriff was *guarding* the lane! It would be easy enough to do; the streets became very narrow and twisted in this quarter. Pulling back against the shaded wall, Jacques looked past the lawman into the passageway and saw a throng of rich merchants, Gilbert and Monsieur Pradet, the jewelry importer, among them. They stood unmoving, silently looking up at the gargoyle protruding from the high roof of the jewelers' guildhall.

Suddenly a puff of white smoke blew out of the monster's mouth, and a low howl emanated from between its sharp stone fangs. The merchants below gasped and fell to their knees as a long red tongue slithered out of the statue and a rumbling voice proclaimed, "I am Gurawl, god of the seven-pointed star, come to reward you for your reverence and devotion! Heed my messenger!"

From the narrow flat area behind the gargoyle rose a majestic figure, its black cloak billowing in the breeze, full against the gray slate roof that rose to a point behind him. Its hideous crimson face, partly hidden by a dark hood, clearly matched that of the gargoyle below. "The great Gurawl speaks through me to you, on this day of miracles! The great Gurawl works through me to grant you riches beyond imagining, on this night of miracles! Prepare yourselves and your offerings, Sect of the Seven-Pointed Star!"

"Gurawl . . . Gilbert used that name!" thought Jacques. "But that guy on the roof's no god! He's just a 'messenger'! And I'm going to check the 'messenger' out!" He backed his way out of the dark alley, then ran through the twisted lanes until he came out behind the guildhall. There was not a single soul anywhere on his route; Jacques's feeling of unease returned, redoubled. But a scaffold had been erected along the back wall of the hall, and he found the climbing easy, despite his sore wrist.

As he came over the rear of the roof, he could hear the gargoyle's emissary on the other side of the roof's peak, still focused on the men who stood below him at the front of the hall. "Gurawl summons you to the secret meeting place at the rising of the full moon, which none shall see. But you shall see the secret of the ages unfold before your very eyes, as your master and mine

56

rewards those who know him and his works. Tell no one, not your wives and not your children, but—''

All at once his words were interrupted as a shout arose from the crowd. ''Son of the evil one! Cursed seed!'' Jacques had been spotted as he crept over the roof's peak, and many hands pointed upward at him urgently. The emissary swung around and in one quick movement raked his cape across Jacques's eyes. The boy, trying to dodge, lost his balance on the sloping roof instead, and pitched forward. But he reacted immediately, grabbing at the heavy fabric and yanking the monster to his knees. The two of them ended up perched on the narrow flat area behind the stone gargoyle, with thirty feet of emptiness ahead of them.

As the merchants stared in stunned silence, the two rolled to the very edge of the roof, shoving and kicking, enveloped in the black cloak. Jacques freed himself from the tangle and sprawled behind the stone gargoyle. The caped figure scrambled up the sloping roof, but his escape was cut short by the boy, who grabbed the cloak again and pulled him back down.

A heavy black boot kicked hard at Jacques's grasp, connecting solidly with his strained left wrist. He yelled in pain as his grip was broken; for a second, he was afraid this time his wrist was broken. And in that second, another kick sent Jacques pitching over the stone gargoyle into the abyss!

But a thrust of his leg caught the edge of the roof, and his strong right hand grabbed the open mouth of the statue. The world whirled around him, but he came to a halt, hanging over the street. If the man in the cloak came after him now, to finish the job, there would be nothing Jacques could do to stop him. But the gargoyle's emissary was once more scrambling up the roof to make his escape. Jacques stayed where he was, suspended but alive.

He could smell the wood ash that was still smoldering in the hollow drain of the gargoyle. If that guy really *had* been working for such a monster, this one was doing precious little to help the cause.

Meanwhile, from below, the shouts increased in volume. "We'll get you, Jacques Fouché, and the wizard you call Father! You won't stop us, and you won't stop the power of Gurawl!"

Slowly, gingerly, Jacques pulled himself back to safety. Once he got his footing, he went up the sloping roof, following the path of the emissary but seeing no further sign of him. On the back side, he eyed the scaffolding, but he knew better than to descend there, with the dangerous crowd nearby. So he hurried over the neighboring rooftops, grateful that houses in this time were built so close together. And finally, when he felt safe, he swung to a high branch of a shade tree and made his way back to the ground.

Ten

"EN GARDE!" THE YOUNG PAGE WITH THE TOY SWORD CHAL-
lenged his opponent, a wooden post stuck in the hard
dirt of the castle courtyard. He appeared to be about ten
years old, and on his cherubic face was a look of stern
determination. His colorful tunic swished forcefully in
the breeze as he danced around, slashing at the immobile
enemy. "Take that, you culprit!"

Marie stood behind him and watched with amusement
for some moments before interrupting the boy's serious
play. "Excuse me, but I am looking for Lady Chantal
de Boudinel. Can you tell me where she might be?"

The page turned to her and said with a bow, "Yes,
of course, mademoiselle, she is my mother, and I would
be honored to accompany you to her."

Marie suppressed a smile and answered, "Such chiv-
alry, young sir, would make your parents proud. You
have learned your lessons well!"

She followed him through an arched portal and down
a short passage into the great hall of the Château Comtal. The huge room was carpeted with rushes that hid

the scraps of food and bones left for the dogs after the noon meal. Tables were set up near the hearth, and several servants were beginning to prepare them for the early evening feast. The smell of roasting meat and baking bread drifted through the room from the kitchen.

Marie looked around in awe as light streaming through the high windows fell on beautiful tapestries decorating the stone walls. Trophy heads of hunted beasts and dusty shields of ancient knights added to the feeling that this was everything a castle should be—as far beyond Madame Dupuis's house as it was beyond Philippe Fouché's scriptorium. The modern-day Mary and medieval Marie were of one mind here—admiring.

Meanwhile the page was leading her to an alcove where a juggler was entertaining a group of women and children.

"You came to visit!" squealed a delighted Aurelie, running over to hug Marie. "Come and watch the juggler."

The page was not about to relinquish his charge, however, especially not to his little sister. "This person has come to visit Lady Chantal de Boudinel!" he announced importantly. "Not you!"

Aurelie screwed up her face at her brother, who glared back at her fiercely.

"Now, children, now, now," scolded their mother, bustling over, veils flowing.

Lady Chantal's plump figure appeared even rounder in her full gown, and the several layers of delicate material she draped over her shoulders. A fine white cloth covered her head and one called a wimple swaddled her neck, no doubt hiding a triple chin. Her twinkling blue

60

eyes and rosy cheeks reminded Marie of a fairy god-mother from childhood stories.

"Thank you, Florian, for guiding our visitor. The viscount will be very proud of your performance, and I am very proud of you, as well." She gave him a loving pat on the back as he turned to leave, and then said to her daughter, "Aurelie, go see what the juggler is doing now."

As the little girl skipped back to the performance, Lady Chantal turned to her visitor and smiled. It was a very formal smile. "Are you certain you wished to see *me*, girl?"

Marie curtsied very low and said, "Madame Dupuis sent me to you, milady."

"Really? Whyever for?" inquired Lady Chantal.

"She said that you might be able to give me some information about a mysterious cult in the area."

Lady Chantal's formality showed a crack. "The cult . . ." She took an imperious look around and made certain they were alone. "I wouldn't ordinarily traffic in such gossip, you understand—especially with the lower classes—but since Madame Dupuis sent you. . . ." The glint in the lady's eye gave the lie to that little speech; Marie knew she could hardly wait to pass it on. "We have only been lodging at the castle for two weeks so far this season, and already I seem to be the authority on local rumors. I seldom hear about such things when I am at our home in the country. Now, let me see . . ." Lady Chantal closed her eyes and sorted through her mental file of information. "Evil magic and dark doings," she said slowly. "Yes . . . and a monster god drooling fiery lava!" Her eyes popped open as she looked to see what effect her revelations had on the innocent looking girl.

"Monster god?" Marie's modern mind knew that superstition was rampant in the Middle Ages. "In Carcassonne?"

"It could be *anywhere*. Watch out!" The lady warmed to her subject. "Terrible things can happen! This cult has great power with the help of this evil force. I've heard that great wealth is involved; ill-gotten wealth I'd wager. Some people would trade their souls for diamonds and gold. But apparently only very rich gentlemen are members." She quickly glanced over her shoulder again, and then whispered conspiratorially to Marie, "I wouldn't be surprised if some of the people in this very castle were a part of it. Some say even the viscount has his hand in!" She pulled back, blinking rapidly. "I wonder why *we* weren't invited." For a moment her brow knit as she dwelt on this slight. Then she returned to her subject with renewed fervor. "The latest I've heard is that one of the town's scribes is involved somehow, which doesn't seem at all fair. Those calligraphers can't make much money."

Marie stepped forward, shocked. "A scribe? Who?"

"I don't know which one, but my dear friend, Lady Simone, spoke of it this morning." She lowered her voice and a giggle slipped out. "And what do you think about Lady Simone? I have just been told that she plans to wave her handkerchief at the tournament for that handsome knight, Sir Étienne."

But Marie heard nothing of this latest gossip, shaken by the words that came before it.

"A scribe?" she thought. "Could it be that Louis is

62

involved in the strange cult? Although I dislike the man, I didn't think of him as evil." But that wasn't what was shaking her, of course. Despite her efforts to bury her other thought, the idea that Lady Chantal could be talking about her father refused to disappear. After all, what did she, Mary Chamness, really know about Philippe Fouché, a man 700 years removed in time? A man with a secret room?

But Marie Fouché knew he was her father.

As soon as she could make her excuses, Marie left Lady Chantal and struck out for the scriptorium, where she was to rendezvous with her brother and François. She'd gained some information, but she knew there were many pieces still missing from the complete picture, and she hoped the other two would have them.

Especially the piece that would reassure her that her father was not part of the evil that hung over this town.

Eleven

JACQUES TRIED TO CALM HIMSELF AS HE SLIPPED THROUGH the quiet alleys toward the cathedral where he was to meet François. Though he was back in the land of brighter sunshine, he was still shaken by his fight with the gargoyle's messenger. His wrist was swollen and throbbing, and since winter had ended over a month before, he knew there was no possibility of finding ice for it. He would just have to ignore it the rest of the way. But what he could not ignore were the accusations the merchants had made, that his father was an evil man.

"Of course, it can't be true," thought Jacques, "but why would they say such a thing?" The boy knew Philippe was a good man; he felt that instinctively. Still . . . what about his secret room? And what was his connection with the magic poem that had brought the twins here in the first place? If there *were* wizardry involved, then there *could* be a gargoyle god, and that was a lot more than he'd bargained for when he'd begun this adventure. Still, he was in no mood to quit—not even when the cathedral came into view. The cathedral with the gargoyles on its roof . . .

Jacques hurried up the steps and entered the cathedral beneath the monsters' cold stone gazes. No emissaries appeared to stop him; there was only the chanting of priests at prayer, echoing off the walls of the majestic interior. Rays of late afternoon sunlight passed through the beautiful stained-glass windows, scattering hundreds of tiny rainbows throughout the building.

Jacques quietly walked up the aisles, looking into the pews and small alcoves for his friend. After searching without success for many minutes, growing ever more anxious for the younger boy's safety, he peeked into the confessional booth. There he was, sound asleep!

Jacques said, in a deep and resonant voice, "Waiting to have your sins forgiven, my son?"

François jolted upright, then realized who'd awakened him. "Don't scare me like that!" he hissed. He struggled to regain his composure, finally adding, "Besides, this is a holy place. You're not supposed to make jokes about sins."

"Sorry, François, you're right. It's just that we're in a tough situation, and I was trying to lighten it up."

Jacques did look very serious, so François immediately recovered his own good humor. "Hey, don't worry about it. Sometimes funny things do happen in church." He smiled. "Just after I got here, I was hiding in the front pew when I saw Father Joseph hurrying down the side aisle. He looked really mad!" He began to giggle at the memory of the roly-poly priest with bushy eyebrows, rosy cheeks, and a mouth stretched wide in outrage.

"He was heading for that old hermit Renard, who

looked like he was dipping things in the holy water. Kind of messy, splashing it all around.'' For a moment he couldn't go on, his lips tight and his freckled cheeks full of air, as he tried to stifle his laughter.

''When Renard saw Father Joseph, he grabbed his little bag and took off toward the side door. But it was locked, so he ran through that row of pews to get to the middle aisle.'' François was pointing with one hand and clutching Jacques shoulder with the other.

''Then Father Joseph *jumped* over that side bench, *I'm not kidding,* and chased the old guy all the way outside. I guess he didn't catch him, 'cause he just came right back in. But I've never seen him look so mad!''

Jacques laughed, but at the same time he grabbed the soccer ball from the floor of the booth and handed it to the younger boy. ''Let's go,'' he said. ''I hope Marie's back at our house already. And I *sure* hope my father's home when we get there! We have a lot to talk about.''

The boys descended the stone steps in front of the church, looking around—and in Jacques's case, upward—carefully. They had just reached the small square across the road when they heard a shout.

''What do you two think you're doing here? This is our neighborhood!'' Vincent, Louis the scribe's apprentice, and two bigger boys were just coming around the side of a nearby building.

Jacques glared at the boys as they quickly surrounded him and François. ''Just back off, twerp. We're not planning to stick around!'' Jacques said.

''Is that so?'' snarled the biggest boy, Martin, grabbing the soccer ball from François. He tossed it to Vincent, who then threw it to the third boy, Denis.

"Give it back!" shouted François. He darted toward Denis who lifted the ball high over his head.

"Too bad you're so short, walnut!" the bully taunted as the smaller boy tried to jump for the ball. Martin and Vincent laughed uproariously and pointed at the spectacle while Jacques coolly considered his options.

François retreated a few steps and glowered at his tormenter. He was also considering his options. Suddenly he bent over and started running, ramming his head into the other boy's stomach.

"Oof!!!" Denis dropped the ball and doubled over, his breath knocked out of him.

Jacques made a quick dash and, with a flick of his right foot, kicked the ball to François. Now François's small size was an advantage as he darted past the lumbering Martin, skillfully dribbling away from the group.

Jacques took off after him but was thrown to the ground and pinned by the biggest bully. Then Vincent sat on his back and began to pull his hair, as Jacques bucked and began to pound Vincent's legs with his fists. Vincent started yelling, "Get him, somebody!"

Denis had recovered and grabbed Jacques's right hand. "I know just the way to put you out of work, scribe!" he threatened, grinning evilly as he began to bend back Jacques's fingers.

Then a horsewhip cracked over their heads, and a strong voice commanded, "Let him go!"

Standing up in his cart, Benjamin, the Dupuis's servant, scowled at the toughs. "Three against one isn't fair, you know." He raised his whip at them. "Get off with you, you scoundrels!"

The three ruffians stared insolently at the man, refusing to budge.

Crack! The whip snapped again, this time inches from their eyes.

They sprang to their feet and moved out of range. All three boys knew only too well the sting of a whip; Louis was not above enforcing his discipline in that manner. Throwing a final sneer at Jacques—but not Benjamin—they turned their backs and sauntered away.

"What is this world coming to when a person can't walk the streets in safety?" Benjamin muttered, shaking his head sadly as he watched the bullies stroll away. "Are you all right, son?" He jumped down from the cart and offered his hand to Jacques, who accepted it gratefully.

"Thank you, Benjamin. I don't think I could have gotten out of that one by myself," said the boy, brushing the dirt from his tunic.

"Makes me shudder to think about breaking anybody's fingers," replied Benjamin, suiting action to his words. Now that the action was over, the whip quivered nervously in his hands. "Take care, Jacques. I don't know what this town's coming to, really I don't. In the old days, that sort of thing would *never* have happened. These kids today . . ." Continuing his reminiscences, he climbed back into the cart, waved to Jacques, and rode off down the street. Jacques was left smiling, and remembering that the proverb "The more things change, the more they stay the same" comes from the French.

Then he remembered everything else, and the smile went away.

Twelve

ON HER WAY HOME, MARIE DUCKED INTO THE BREAD SHOP where Josiane worked. Her mind was as occupied with their mystery as her brother's, but unlike Jacques, she also remembered that all they'd eaten today was almonds, and she was prepared to do something about it.

"One baguette, please, Josiane," Marie said to the teenager, "and also one of your special round loaves. My father's favorite."

"Certainly, Marie." Josiane reached for the bread, saying, "Jacques looked a bit surprised to see me this afternoon. I've never seen him blush in that particular bright shade of scarlet." She chuckled at the memory. "Still . . . that's part of his charm. One day a sophisticated man of the world, and the next, an embarrassed little boy."

Marie tried to imagine her twin as a sophisticated man of the world, and laughed. "That's Jacques, all right, afloat between two worlds." As she handed Josiane some coins, she added mentally, "You don't know the half of it!"

She left the shop and hurried off toward the rendez-vous. Rounding the corner by the butcher shop, she nearly collided with the Italian troubadour.

"Oh! Excuse me," she gasped, looking up into a pair of soft brown eyes.

"No, no, it's my fault," replied the singer. "My mind was in the clouds." His accent, like his smile, was just as charming as his eyes.

"You're the troubadour, aren't you? The one I heard singing *The Song of Roland* earlier this afternoon?" ventured the girl, her cheeks reddening despite herself.

"Ah, I am reluctant to call myself a troubadour, ma-demoiselle. I'm not nearly so highborn as most of them are. As a *minstrel,* I sing, I play the mandolin, and I travel; nothing more."

"You have come to entertain the tournament crowds?" Marie asked.

The young man nodded and put his bag on the ground. Holding out his hand, he said, "My name is Antonio. What's yours?"

Marie shifted the bread to her left side and shook his hand. "I am Marie. Welcome to our town."

After a long silent moment, Antonio gently released her hand and asked, "May I walk with you?"

"Oh, uh-uh . . . no." Now she was stammering, just as Jacques had with Josiane; what a wimp she was! "It's not possible just now. I have . . . important busi-ness, and must hurry home. But thank you, perhaps an-other time."

She rushed past him with a quick goodbye. When she reached the curve of the stone passage, Marie glanced back over her shoulder to see Antonio watching her curiously. She waved to him and then quickly ran the final block to home and the scriptorium.

She was concentrating hard on her experiences of the afternoon, trying to make sense of the deluge of details filling her brain. And her heart was filled with worry for Henri. She was so distracted that she didn't notice the shadow coming from behind—until it was too late.

Two hands grabbed her, one of them clamped over her mouth, stifling her scream; and the other hard around her waist. She tried to twist around out of her captor's grasp, but found herself in a tighter clinch as she was dragged into a narrow alley nearby.

Marie frantically tried to remember all of those self-defense hints she'd read about in magazines back home. She regained her footing and tried to stomp on her attacker's instep, but was prevented as her long dress only tangled more around her legs. Her right hand pulled at the grip covering her mouth, but his hands were powerful and wouldn't be budged.

Then with all the force she could muster, Marie drove her free elbow back into her attacker, striking the soft area just below the ribs. Kind of like a Heimlich maneuver, only to save *her* life, not the recipient's.

She knocked the breath out of him, and immediately felt some loosening of his grip. Ducking low, she managed to squeeze out and around, pushing hard to separate herself from the man. But was it a man? . . . or a monster!?

She was staring at an incredibly horrible face, a face more animal than human—the face of a gargoyle! The face of the monster god, with long pointed teeth bracketing a gaping black hole from which its red tongue

71

dangled. The creature struggled to catch its breath, a thick wheezing noise coming from behind its protruding crimson snout, as its two eyes, shrouded beneath a dark hood, glared at her fiercely. Two eyes . . . from behind a mask! It was a *man,* not a god! But that was small comfort as the man backhanded her across the face.

Marie felt a scream explode, escaping with such ferocious energy it seemed to push her back. She stumbled into the road. A shutter flew open and a woman's voice shouted, "What's going on?" Two houses down, a young man peeked warily from his doorway, holding a knife.

But Marie, unable to speak, could only point to the now-empty alley. Her attacker had fled rather than be seen.

Suddenly she heard more footsteps behind her. It was Jacques and François, racing toward her. "What happened? We heard you screaming!" shouted Jacques. "Are you okay?"

His sister nodded breathlessly, but taking hold of Jacques's arm, turned to her curious neighbors and said in what was a reasonable attempt at a reasonable voice, "Sorry to alarm you. It was all a mistake. I got scared by a shadow. Go home now." Her face was strained, but Jacques knew better than to press her for an explanation in public. He held his tongue until they arrived home and Marie unlocked the scriptorium door. He and François followed her inside.

"Someone did attack me," she said to them then. "Someone wearing a blood-red gargoyle mask! It must be connected to Henri's disappearance. We've got to . . ." She broke off, her eye caught by a scrap of parchment just inside the doorway. She bent down to pick it up, and recognized it immediately. It was a message almost identical to the one left in Henri's studio.

"Do not seek your father or he will die! Be silent, and he shall return unharmed in two days' time."

Tears filled her eyes as concern for Philippe overcame her. There was no longer any question: He *was* her father, just as surely as her twentieth-century father was, and she loved him. *Who* could be doing this to him? She handed the message to her brother, saying, "Now they've got them both."

Jacques's face turned white and the muscle along his jaw twitched. "They won't get away with it! We are going to figure this out *now*!" he snapped with fierce determination. "You say the man who attacked you was wearing a gargoyle mask! Tell me all about that."

So Marie told the boys about the man in the dark cloak who had followed her, and the man in the crimson mask who attacked her (the same man?). She told about her visits to the aristocratic ladies, the rumor of a scribe's involvement, the monster god, and Monsieur Dupuis's odd behavior. Her brother then filled them in on his own battle with the creature on the roof, who was almost certainly the man who'd attacked Marie. He also told of his captivity in the wineshop, and the merchants' accusations about their father. François looked on amazed, and perhaps, once more, a little fearful. But when the twins had finished their recitals, François was the first to ask a question.

"I wonder why this place wasn't searched," he said, looking around the room. "Perhaps they don't know the pages we have were missing from the book."

"More likely, they just couldn't break in without attracting attention," responded Jacques. "Since Henri's burglar last week, we've been extra careful about locking up."

He thought hard for a moment, then looked at Marie. "Listen, I know we're not supposed to look in Father's secret room, but right now I don't think we have a choice. If a scribe really is mixed up in all of this, we've got to find out if it's Father."

"It's not," she said quickly.

"I know—but we have to be sure."

Marie grudgingly gave her agreement, and the twins hurried toward the stairs. François hung back for a moment, his heart thumping in an otherwise frozen body. Secret room? But he sure didn't want to stay downstairs by himself, so he quickly bounded up after his friends.

Jacques was the first to reach the door on the top floor. "We're going to have to bust it down," he said, testing its solidity with a thump of his shoulder.

Suddenly Marie clutched his other shoulder. "Shh!" she whispered urgently. "I heard something downstairs!" The three kids stood stock-still, straining hard in the dead silence to hear the sound again—then trembled all at once when they heard the unmistakable *chunk* of the heavy door closing.

"Father!" murmured Marie hopefully, starting forward. But her descent of the stairs was halted by her brother's firm hand.

"We don't know that!" said Jacques in a forceful whisper. Though two floors lay between them and the workshop, they couldn't risk being detected. "It could be anybody. I didn't lock the door, because we're here."

"Oh, good one, bro!" she muttered. But her heart wasn't in it; her heart was in her mouth.

The three friends tiptoed carefully back down to the bedroom, across the floor, and down another flight of stairs. In the solar they moved even more carefully, avoiding the rushes that would surely have crackled and announced their presence. They came to a halt at the top of the next staircase, listening carefully to the sounds from the floor below. To the kids' amazement, they seemed to be the sounds of shuffling parchment, and the gentle clinking of an ink pot. Maybe it *was* their father.

They had left the sitting-room door open when they hurried upstairs, so now, by squatting and peeking around the doorjamb, Jacques could see the man in the studio below. It *was* a calligrapher—but it wasn't Philippe.

"Louis!" the boy exclaimed, unable to stop himself. The scribe's head jerked up like a fox's in a henhouse and stared straight at Jacques, who was staring at him. In the next instant, Louis bolted to the door, flung it open, and dashed out. The two boys were down the stairs and after him in a flash, but when they erupted onto the narrow street, the scribe had vanished into thin air.

Magic?

Meanwhile, in the workshop, Marie was trying to blot up ink that had spilled and stained the bottom edge of one of the pages she had proofread earlier that day. But it was the neatly applied fresh ink at the top of the page that caused her to cry out in fury. "Hey! This says 'dohimus,' not 'dominus' like it's supposed to! It was okay when I checked it before!" She quickly scanned the rest. "And here's 'allehiia' where it should be 'alleluia'!" She was livid. The similarity of angular strokes in the Gothic alphabet had made the alterations hardly noticeable, but Marie was a professional proofreader. "Louis was trying to make Father look incompetent!"

"Maybe he stole Henri's silver-leaf sheets to mess *him* up, too!" said François excitedly. "Maybe even the manuscript pages!"

"Maybe even the calligraphers!" added Marie breathlessly.

"Wait a minute. Let's think about this," said Jacques. "We know he wants their business, but would he go so far as to kidnap them? That's a long stretch from dirty tricks. And I just can't picture him coming back here to botch some lettering if he's committed a far more serious crime."

François, standing in the doorway, noticed something by his toe. "Look at this. It's a clod of red dirt." He picked up the crumbly pellet, examining it thoughtfully, but it was Marie who spoke next. "Jacques—do you remember? We saw dirt just like that at Henri's today!"

"Dirt? At Henri's?" asked François. "There was none when I swept up this morning."

"I'll be darned!" said Jacques. "An actual clue! Only . . . what does it mean?"

"There are some caves just outside the south gate, down close to the river," answered François excitedly. "When I was a small boy, I used to play there while my father fished. One of the caves is well hidden . . . it was my special place. My mother didn't like me to play there because the red dirt stuck to my clothes."

"You're right!" said Jacques. "I've been there!"

Marie jumped up excitedly. "Sure we have! We all have! Let's go!" she almost shouted. "I'll bet that's where the kidnappers have taken Father and Henri!"

"Maybe we should get the sheriff to go with us," suggested François.

Jacques shook his head and told them about the sheriff. "We're on our own," the boy said grimly.

The three kids quickly locked the door and ran toward the south gate.

Thirteen

MARCEL, THE KEEPER OF THE SOUTHERN GATE IN CAR-cassonne's high stone walls, looked at the young people suspiciously. "It's nearly sundown! You children shouldn't be out so late," he said. "What would your father think? It's not at all safe!"

"Don't worry, Marcel. We'll be careful, and we won't be too late," said Marie gently, trying to calm the old man. "Besides, Jacques and I are thirteen now. You needn't consider us children."

"I suppose. . . . But the comings and goings these evenings have kept me busy, all right. It must be the new alehouse that has opened up down the road." He winked at the kids. "You're not going there, are you?"

They laughed and shook their heads. "No, Marcel. We'll be back soon," said Jacques, pulling the other two along with him.

They hurried down the road as the last traces of the sun streaked orange and teal across the darkening sky. In the dying light, they found the small cart path turning off to the right, leading down to the caves. The path, they noted happily, showed an unusual amount of recent activity.

"It's over here a bit," said François, leading the way.

The rushing sound of the river Aude could be heard on the left, and some raucous laughter from the tavern on the main road drifted through the cool evening air. They ran down the path, kicking up the red dust, and then cut off and wound through bushes. It was getting quite dark now, and the moon had yet to rise. They could barely see, but all three remembered the route to the secret cave. With an occasional barked shin, they reached it fairly quickly. Only then, when they were congratulating themselves on their abilities to navigate in near darkness, did they realize that they next had to enter pitch darkness—and in their haste, they'd forgotten to bring a torch.

"'The secret meeting place, at the rising of the full moon which none shall see,'" muttered Jacques. "He was talking about being in a cave!"

"What?" asked Marie.

"This *is* the place! C'mon—we can feel our way," replied her brother excitedly, leading the other two into the damp blackness. "Just hold hands and don't let go."

"Sure," said Marie, with a heartiness she didn't really feel. "After all, we've been here before. . . ."

They crept down the mazelike passage, feeling along the cold rock wall. The real Jacques and Marie's memories assured the twins that there were no pitfalls or dropoffs ahead of them, but there were outcroppings just waiting to clip the head or shoulder of anyone who got too confident. Winding left, then right, they went deeper into the cave.

Something whooshed past Marie's ear, and she trembled at the sensation. *"Plecotus auritus!"* she whispered.

"What?!" asked François sharply, imagining monsters with a name like that. He was only slightly relieved when she clarified, "Bats!" Jacques squeezed his hand to comfort him.

But all at once, Marie realized that the absolute blackness had become somewhat less absolute. "Look!" she whispered. "There's some sort of light ahead!"

"Yeah," breathed Jacques. "Pretty dim, but there must be someone around a corner with a torch!"

Stealthily they moved on toward the light, when, suddenly, they heard the sound of pounding feet not far behind them. For a moment they stood frozen, caught between two possible evils—then François was dragging the other two around the next bend. Wordlessly, he pointed toward a narrow break in the opposite wall. It was barely wide enough for a grown man to enter, but it was visible in the cave's twilight, and it was the answer to their prayers.

One after the other, they bolted into the opening, and back into darkness. As soon as Jacques brought up the rear, they slowed and felt their way again. As quickly but as silently as they could, they moved farther down the narrow corridor, praying they wouldn't be discovered. Outside, the footfalls grew in volume, then receded.

"Whoa!" The exclamation was out of François's mouth before he could think to stifle it. He had nearly fallen into a large pit, where the path before them gave way abruptly. Marie's grip on him tightened instinctively as she pulled him back from the precipice.

The three kids crouched in tense silence, scarcely daring to breathe, but the footsteps didn't come back. Evidently no one else had heard François cry out.

"I had forgotten about this hole!" whispered the young apprentice, shaken and somewhat ashamed. "But I remember, now, nearly falling in when I was little."

From below them, a low moan rose from the abyss.

Fourteen

THE THREE KIDS FROZE, GRIPPING ONE ANOTHER MORE tightly. The moan came again, stronger this time. Marie felt every strand of her golden hair stand on end. But she eased herself closer to the edge.

"Who's down there?" she whispered, trying to focus her voice only on the pit. It still sounded agonizingly loud in the enclosed passageway.

Her only answer was another wordless noise, but one with a purpose equal to hers.

"Father?" she called. "Henri?"

Another sound, even more forceful.

"It's Marie, Jacques, and François. You sound gagged. Groan once for yes and twice for no, but not too loudly. We think there are people in another part of the cave. Is either of you hurt?"

Two groans. No.

"Are you tied up?"

One groan. Yes.

"We're going to find a way to get you out of there. Can you hold on for a short time while we look around?"

Again a solitary groan signaled yes.

"We'll be back," whispered Jacques, leading the way back out of the tunnel.

The friends made their way back to the main passageway, then turned toward the glow of light, deeper into the cave. Now they could hear confused sounds coming from the same direction.

The passage opened into a large cavern lit by one torch at the farside. Beneath an iridescent painting of a seven-pointed star, the man in the gargoyle mask held his audience of merchants spellbound, proclaiming, "Our god, Gurawl, will protect us from the wicked spells cast by the evil magician, Philippe Fouché!" Jacques and Marie recoiled at these words as if from a blow, but kept their presence undetected as they crept behind a large outcropping of stalagmites.

The masked man was continuing: "On Sunday last, you witnessed the multiplication of one simple pearl necklace. At this hour, with my magical energy and the power of our god, you will see the gold coins on the altar before you reproduce once—twice—many times!"

Uttering a magical incantation, the man before them lit a small torch, which he placed into a holder on a multilayered altar . . . and then a collective gasp, redolent with greed, filled the room as the pile of coins became two piles! He intoned another chant and lit another torch, and the two piles became four! Once more, and the piles doubled again!

"Wealth! Wealth as you've never known it before!" cried the man in the crimson mask, his arms extended toward the treasure.

From their hidden vantage point, the kids could hardly

believe their eyes. But a brooding frown slid over Jacques's face.

"Something is wrong with those coins," he said, straining to see the altar through the flickering and uncertain torchlight.

Suddenly he grasped his sister's arm hard enough to make her cry out, if she'd had lesser self-control. As it was, she bit her lip as he whispered excitedly, "I knew it! That fraud's using mirrors! The largest stack of coins is on the left in the original pile, but on the right in the second, and then they alternate!"

"Of course," answered Marie, seeing it at once. "Reflections, and reflections of reflections!"

"He's no more magic than we are!" said Jacques, not entirely unrelieved at learning the truth.

"All is in readiness! Bring your jewels to me in two hours' time, and you will become rich beyond your dreams!" the fake conjurer commanded his audience. As one, without argument, they stood up and began to make their way back the way they'd come. Which meant the kids had to do the same, and quickly.

Jacques led the way, creeping from the cavern, then they ran back down into the smaller side passage. They stood in darkness and watched the merchants tramping out of the cave, so close they could have reached out and touched them. They did not see the man in the mask.

"We're alone in here with him," whispered Marie.

"Not *that* alone," said her brother. "Remember Father and Henri." He turned to François. "How deep would you say that pit is?"

"I don't know . . . maybe eight feet?"

"That's about the way I remember it." He grinned, though no one could see him in the dark. "This looks like my day for holes in the ground."

He felt his way to the edge of the pit and called down to the men below. The answering sounds told him where they were. He made his way to one side so he wouldn't land on them, and then, while Marie and François waited anxiously, carefully lowered himself over the edge. Stretched out fully, he released his grip, falling the last few feet to the bottom.

A nearby groan led him to his father. Quickly he removed the man's gag and cut the ropes that bound him.

"Thank God, you're all right!" whispered Jacques, giving Philippe a big hug.

"I can say the same to you, Jacques," croaked Philippe through parched lips. "You had no idea what you were up against."

"Tell me while I untie Henri." At the rim of the pit, the other kids strained to hear.

"It started with rumors," Philippe whispered, stretching so hard that his joints cracked—an unsettling sound with the enemy not so very far away. He hurried on. "Wherever I went in Carcassonne, I heard a little bit here, a little bit there. Something was growing beneath the town's normal façade—something unhealthy. I saw men wearing a seven-pointed star. I overheard snippets of a conversation between Old Gilbert, the wine merchant, and his wife . . . and the words 'magic' and 'wealth beyond dreams' and 'the god of gargoyles.' I decided to ask Gilbert what he meant. That was my mistake." Philippe sighed. "He told me he was just

85

discussing a tale he'd heard, and I pretended to believe him. The problem was, he was only pretending to believe *me*. I went to Henri, the one man I'm sure I can trust, and asked him to draw the clues I'd discovered into the margins of Madame Dupuis's Book of Hours, in case I . . . disappeared. I thought the pages were safe at Henri's, but he tells me most of them were stolen when he was waylaid this morning.''

"So when Gilbert calls you an 'evil wizard' . . .'' Marie began.

"That's what the man in the gargoyle mask told Gilbert and the others, so they'd come after me. He claims to be a wizard, so he calls his enemies wizards, too.''

By now Henri was free of his bonds. The illustrator rubbed his sore wrists and ankles and sighed. "Enough talk, Philippe. Let's get out of this pit!''

"Quickly, before that devil comes back!'' said Jacques, bending to give the two men a boost up.

But Marie's whisper came urgently from above: "Wait! Maybe you should stay here for now.''

"What?'' answered Henri. "Are you insane?'' He turned toward Philippe. "Is your daughter insane?''

"Sometimes I think so,'' said Philippe, "but all fathers do.''

"Listen to me,'' Marie replied, and quickly told them what had happened in the large cavern. "If you escape now, we'll lose our best chance for capturing and unmasking the leader of the sect. They'll all fade back into their day jobs if they find you gone. Worse than that, Father will still be a suspect.''

"She's right,'' said Philippe. "Very good, Marie. We have to catch this criminal in the act.''

"I *suppose* you're right . . . " admitted Henri, who sounded like he supposed anything *but* that.

Philippe had already turned his mind to the problem confronting them. "We can reposition our gags. Even with a torch, the light down here won't be enough to show our captor we've been untied."

"I have an idea," said Jacques. "This is what we'll do. . . ."

Fifteen

P HILIPPE HOISTED HIS SON TO HIS SHOULDERS, AND J ACQUES pulled himself out of the hole.

"We have to hurry!" he said to Marie and François. The three friends held hands and walked quickly back to the main passageway, then to the cave's exit. This trip was easier than before because the full moon had risen, throwing soft gray light into the cave opening. They rushed out into the fresh air and smack into the arms of a tall man in a black hooded cloak. Marie knew him at once as the man who'd tried to follow her in town. Instinctively she drew a breath to scream.

But the hooded man was faster; his hand covered her mouth as he whispered urgently, "I am on your side! Do not be afraid!" Then he drew back his hood to reveal his face. The kids stood goggling at the young minstrel from Italy, Antonio.

"Follow me!" he ordered.

"No way," said Jacques, planting himself firmly. It was just possible that the masked man had passed them while they were conferring in the pit; that the minstrel was the masked man, waiting outside the cave for the merchants to come back. More than the lack of a torch, Jacques now regretted his lack of a weapon. Marie could take care of herself as well as he could, but François couldn't, and François was their responsibility.

Antonio, for his part, saw the situation at a glance and spread his empty hands. "Listen to me. It's time you knew who I am, why I'm here. But come away from the mouth of the cave, or they'll catch us. I'll stay in plain sight, but come with me."

Marie jumped in. "That makes sense, Jacques, whatever Antonio's really doing here. Anyone can come this way at any time."

"All right," said Jacques grudgingly; then, to Antonio, "But don't make any sudden moves."

The foursome made its way by moonlight to a field several hundred feet upriver, where the cattails rose above their heads to form a screen and the murmur of the water masked the sounds of their voices. They could still keep an eye on the cave mouth through the reeds, but it was unlikely anyone would spot them. There the minstrel spoke again.

"Two years ago a man came to my town in Italy. He secretly gathered the richest merchants together and convinced them that he could make them even richer. No one would be hurt, he said, because it would all be accomplished through 'magic.' "

"This sounds familiar," said Marie, grimacing.

Antonio's voice took on an edge of long-held anger. "My father was a good man, but he fell under the spell of this 'magician' and was cheated out of much of his wealth, like all the others. Businesses were ruined, trade faltered, and within three months, the spirit of the town died. Several town leaders, including my father, grew ill from worry and shame, and my father died like his town."

The young man looked fierce in the moonlight. "I had no other family. My mother died when I was born, and my father meant everything to me. I swore that I would find the criminal and bring him to justice. I had no money, but I had my voice, so I set out as a minstrel, able to travel wherever I wished and support myself as I roamed, following any rumor that caught my ear. It has taken me two years, but I have managed to track the man here to Carcassonne."

"So who is he?" demanded Jacques.

"I don't know. I have never known. But I know his works."

"Is that why you followed me? Did you think I would lead you to him?" asked Marie.

"I didn't know what you knew. I had heard someone speaking about your father, 'the evil wizard,' but I was able to make certain that your father hadn't left France in the past three years."

"What brought you to this cave tonight, Antonio?" Jacques asked.

"Since I arrived in town, I've had my eye on Monsieur Pradet, and some of the other leading merchants, as potential victims. When they started leaving their businesses earlier than usual yesterday, I followed them here; it seems to be the sect's usual meeting place. I came back tonight and was considering entering the cave, even though I'd have been at a severe disadvantage not knowing its tunnels, when I saw you three go

90

in. You seemed to know what you were doing, so I waited to see what happened.''

"And if we'd gotten into trouble . . . ?'' Marie asked.

"I'd . . . well, I'd have just blundered in to try to help,'' answered Antonio.

"You *have* helped,'' Marie said. "Since *you* didn't see the man we're all looking for come out of the cave, we know he's still inside.''

The young man's eyes widened, and he took a hasty step toward the cave.

Jacques stopped him. "Don't go. We have to catch him in the act tonight.'' He then explained the mirror trick to them.

Antonio and François were mystified. "But no mirror I've seen can reflect so clearly,'' said the younger boy.

"These are not the polished metal mirrors that are common now. I have studied the matter, and I know that the ancient people in eastern countries made mirrors by applying silver to the backs of sheets of glass. Those mirrors can easily do what we saw tonight.'' Jacques did not explain that he knew this from Mr. Shivan's history class at Skyline Middle School.

He continued: "We have less than two hours to prepare. Let's get back to the scriptorium!''

Sixteen

BACK IN THE WORKSHOP, THE KIDS ASSEMBLED THE SUP-
plies that Jacques said they'd need. Thin sheets of parchment, the box of paints, small brushes, a knife, and a
candle were placed on one of the worktables. There
were also a few twigs and a pile of small rocks they'd
collected on the way back.

"We're going to expose that so-called magician by
breaking his mirrors with slingshots," said Jacques.
"Antonio, I need to borrow a string from your mandolin. It's from animal gut, is that right?"

The minstrel nodded and pulled the mandolin out of
his bag. He untied a string and handed it to the other
boy.

Jacques picked up a Y-shaped stick and tied an end
of the gut string to each arm of the Y. Fitting a stone
into the loop of the string, he pulled it back and then
let the string go. The stone flew about three feet and
clattered to the ground.

"Nuts! I had hoped the gut would be more elastic!"
said Jacques, disappointed.

François was puzzled. "I don't understand the word 'elastic,' and your sling is a strange design. I have another way."

The younger boy untied the string. In a small parchment square, he cut two tiny slits and laced the string through them. He selected a rock and positioned it in the piece of parchment. Holding both ends of the string and whipping his creation around in a circle, he jerked his wrist, sending the stone straight and hard into Antonio's cloak, which hung by the door.

"I've got the best aim in Carcassonne!" he proclaimed proudly.

"Go, François!" laughed Marie, clapping her hands at the display. "What a champ!"

"Gimme five!" said Jacques, raising his hand. He quickly turned this into an awkward handshake when his friend gave him a confused look.

"Antonio, you need to make a mask. Not a crimson one; you want to look magnificent and invincible, but good-hearted." Jacques passed a piece of parchment over to his new friend.

Then he began cutting some shapes out of the other parchment. "Now we'll make some model airplanes, and we have to work quickly, so just follow my example."

"Airplanes?" Antonio and François asked in unison.

Marie frowned at her brother. "I think he means toy birds," she said.

"Exactly!" said Jacques. "Or, maybe, more like toy angels. We're going to wake that crowd up with a swarm of them!"

For the next half hour, the group worked hard cutting

and folding pieces of parchment. With brilliant colors, they painted angelic faces on their flying models. A dab of melted wax added weight to the front tip, allowing them to fly straight and true. Antonio and François were delighted, having never seen anything like this, and the younger boy had to be reminded more than once to keep to his work and stop flying the little planes around the room.

"And for a final touch, how about this?" asked Marie as she used wax to attach a few wisps cut from a feather quill.

"Terrific! That'll freak 'em out for sure!" answered her brother. "But we'll have to leave it at that. We've got to get back to the cave."

"You certainly speak strangely lately, Jacques," said François, as they gathered the sling, rocks, mask, and parchment angels and put them all into Antonio's emptied bag. Then the four young crime fighters stepped out into the moonlit night—and came face to face with Sir Francis.

"I must see your father immediately!" the knight said to Jacques.

The boy barely hesitated before responding, "I'm sorry, sir, but he's not home right now. When I see him, I'll tell him you came by."

Sir Francis would not be turned away so easily. "He missed an appointment with me this afternoon. And I've heard some talk. . . . I have reason to believe he's involved in illegal activities."

"That's horse-pucky!" snapped Marie, unable to contain herself. "You shouldn't believe everything your wife says!"

Sir Francis stared at her, amazed at the rudeness of her remark. The three boys were also astounded, but what they felt was more like admiration. Then, rather than waste any more time in explanation, the four kids darted around the man and raced away, ignoring his calls to stop.

Seventeen

HUDDLED TOGETHER IN THE CATTAIL-RIMMED FIELD NEAR the silent cave, the kids waited for the merchants to return.

"Thank goodness Marcel was asleep at the gate," Marie said softly. "What if he'd wanted to tell our father?"

"Ha!" laughed Jacques. "What if we'd brought him here, *to* our father?"

"*Shh!* I hear them coming!" whispered Antonio.

Indeed, ten silent men were marching up the path in the darkness. They carried no torches, but with the full moon now high in the sky, there was no need for extra light. Everything was crystal clear. The kids easily picked out Monsieur Pradet, Old Gilbert, and the sheriff. Then the procession entered the cave, and the sounds of their making their way down the rock passage drifted across the night air for a few moments before silence returned.

"We didn't have a torch because we flat out forgot it," said Marie. "But I bet they don't have them because the magician knows it'd screw up his mirror trick.''

"Time to move out," said Jacques, stealthily leading the group to the cave entrance. "Remember the plan."

They stayed close to the side of the passage as they wound down to the main cavern. As they neared the second tunnel where they'd left Philippe and Henri, Jacques slowed, obviously thinking of checking in with the men in the pit, but he could hear the midnight meeting getting underway up ahead. Resolutely, Jacques led them onward to their watching place.

Just as before, the crowd of wealthy merchants was assembled across from the gargoyle-masked magician. In front of him was the altar, and on it was a large bowl filled with jewels, sparkling in the lurid torchlight.

The masked man spoke. "Each of you will have a bowl just like this one, filled with diamonds, rubies, and emeralds. After Gurawl, who loves the darkness, multiplies them for you, I, his humble priest, will put out the light for one minute, during which we must all thank him for his bounty."

His powerful voice rumbled through the cave as he began to chant his spell. "On the night of this full Scorpio moon, with the power provided me by our mighty god, Gurawl, and with the strength of the desires of the Sect of the Seven-Pointed Star . . . this immense treasure is yours!" With his torch he lit the other torches on the altar, one after another, and one after another new bowls of glittering stones appeared as if by magic!

A gasp rolled like a wave through the salivating mob. Their normally stolid faces glowed with crazed pleasure as they watched the fortune grow before their eyes.

But suddenly their hopes were shattered. Literally.

François's aim was perfect as he shot stone after smashing stone in rapid succession, directly into the mirrors. One after another, the glass plates burst into fragments, and so did the reflections of the bowls of jewels.

The merchants had no way of knowing what they were seeing. All they knew was their magic treasure was vanishing even more quickly than it had appeared, and their howls of outrage and pain filled the cavern to overflowing. Their masked leader was almost as dumbfounded. And then both leader and mob were plunged into a new realm of confusion as the twins and Antonio flew their "angels" into their midst. From the friends' hiding place, unearthly howls burst forth to fill the cavern with ghastly echoes.

The merchants, flailing away at the *things* soaring around their heads, trying to escape from the wailing that now surrounded them, were in danger of trampling each other in their overriding desire to flee the cave. It was at this point that Antonio, wrapped in his hooded cape and wearing his benevolent mask, stepped forth from his concealment.

"Halt!" he cried with such authority that the merchants did exactly that.

"I have tracked this false conjurer to his lair at last," Antonio intoned, using every trick of the voice his years as a minstrel had taught him. "He plotted to steal your riches, but now he is yours!" He gestured at the thief. "Take him!"

The mob was already prepared to follow a leader. Now they turned as one on the man who had held that position. But the masked man was no fool. With one swift sweep of his arm, he dashed the torches to the ground, and plunged the cavern into darkness.

The townsmen surged toward his position, but stumbled over one another in their confusion. Old Gilbert was the first to get there. He reached for the man and found nothing, then impacted the altar. He ran his hands over the surface frantically, cutting his fingers with the splintered glass and shrieking, "Gone! Gone! The treasure is gone!"

"What about *our* jewels?" someone called harshly.

"That's what I mean!" sobbed Gilbert. "He has them all!" And then: "I thought he was someone else, but he must have been Philippe Fouché!"

"The evil wizard!" someone else echoed as Jacques and Marie cringed.

Several merchants at the rear of the pack, hoping to find *some* answers, lunged for the spot where Antonio had stood, but Antonio had jumped back to safety among his friends. Finding only empty air on all sides, their own shouts and roars filled the cave and the mob fled en masse. And they wasted no time at it.

Once they made their way back to the entrance, the sheriff and the townsmen took several minutes just catching their breath and recovering their composure. Each knew their night's business was nowhere near complete, but out in the pitiless moonlight, each had to calm down and regain his professional stature. Only when they were satisfied that they were once again the leaders of the town, instead of a howling mob, did they set out to search for the criminal who had stolen their jewels. After all, a good businessman can get more jewels, but a reputation can be lost forever.

The four kids, meanwhile, had hurried toward the small side passage, secure in the knowledge that none of the townsmen would venture back into the cave anytime soon. They found Philippe and Henri already out of the pit, waiting for them.

"We heard everything," said Philippe breathlessly. "Let's get out of here! That man has tried to cast suspicion on me, and we must figure out his identity before the mob finds me!"

"Whoever it was knew how to make mirrors. I'll bet it was the thief who stole the silver leaf from Henri's scriptorium last week. He could have applied the silver to sheets of clear glass," said Jacques.

"I'm sure of it," said Marie. "And Monsieur Dupuis is an importer of fine glass, and he has traveled to Italy . . . and he was acting very strangely when I saw him this afternoon."

"He saw the sketches when I showed them to Madame!" exclaimed Philippe. "So he saw the clues in the margins!"

"I'm surprised he wasn't here with the other rich merchants," said Jacques.

"Perhaps he *was* here . . . behind a mask! Yes . . . it's beginning to come together," said Philippe. "We must hurry to the Dupuis home."

Eighteen

DESPITE THE EARLY HOUR, PHILIPPE PULLED HARD AT THE bell rope on the gate, and the loud gongs could have awakened the whole neighborhood. When there was no immediate answer, he pulled it again, harder.

They heard the heavy front door open. Then the flickering light of a candle approached the gate.

"Who's there at this hour?" said Benjamin, rubbing his eyes. His mouth pulled wide in an uncontrollable yawn.

"It is I, Philippe Fouché. We must see Monsieur Dupuis!" said the scribe forcefully.

"It is not possible, monsieur! My master is sleeping," replied the servant stoutly.

"Sleeping, hah! I have reason to believe that Monsieur Dupuis has done me grave wrong."

"You are mistaken! He has done no such thing!"

"And he has stolen the jewels of many men tonight!" said Jacques.

"That is ridiculous. This is a respectable household. Play your jokes in the daytime—"

"What's going on here?" Monsieur Dupuis, pulling his dressing gown around his slim form, was coming out of the house.

"Sir, we believe that you have committed crimes of kidnapping and thievery, as the leader of a so-called cult of magic. And that you have tried to cast the blame on me!" declared Philippe.

"Me? But this is absurd!" replied the gentleman. "How can you believe this?"

"The thief used mirrors of a type only a expert in glass would know. You are the only such expert in the town."

"I don't deal in mirrors. I deal in objects of art and beauty."

"But glass."

"Yes, certainly, glass. That is not a crime!"

"Then there is this: My daughter saw you burying something in your side yard this afternoon, and muttering."

"I—I deny that absolutely!"

"I saw you!" said Marie. "You knelt down, buried something, and you looked like you didn't want anyone to see you."

"I didn't!" Monsieur Dupuis snapped, but he paused to think for a moment. "Listen," he said in a softer tone, "come inside. This is not talk for the whole town to hear."

The accusers entered the home warily, but were met by Madame Dupuis, who had been listening to the noisy conversation. She moved to stand beside her husband and hold his hand. He waited until Benjamin had firmly closed the door to the outside world before he spoke again.

"This is nothing I would care to have repeated," he said in an odd, blustery tone, "but I was . . . using a magic charm." He quickly raised a hand, palm out. "But it was for protection. I was approached by one of this town's leading citizens—I would really rather not reveal his name—to become a member of the cult you speak of. I refused; I have no use for magic, or for secret societies. And as for their preposterous claim of multiplying gold and jewels . . . I am, if I may say so, already rich enough to disregard such fantasies without a second thought.

"But," he continued, "this cult did not take kindly to my decision. Perhaps they simply wanted a bigger name than any of them had—perhaps they just wanted my money. Either way, I began to receive threats—"

"Bertrand!" gasped Madame Dupuis. "You didn't tell me."

"A wife needn't worry her little head about such things," replied Monsieur Dupuis, while Marie ached to kick him in the shins. "In any event, I decided that *if* they indeed had magic at their disposal, I should buy some of my own. The old woodcutter, Renard, has long been rumored to be a spirit-man. I contacted him and procured a charm—"

"Dipped in holy water!" exclaimed François.

"I saw you get it from him," added Marie. "This afternoon, in the alley."

"Yes, that's right. I was to bury it beneath a rosebush and speak words Renard gave me—a lot of gibberish,

103

if you ask me—before the moon rose, to keep my house and all its occupants safe.''

''Yes, Renard does practice the old ways,'' said Philippe. ''But that still doesn't prove anything. I would like your permission, monsieur, to search your home for the missing jewels.''

Monsieur Dupuis shook his head. ''No, monsieur. I refuse.'' His surprise had finally faded and turned to indignity. ''You cannot presume to awaken my household in the middle of the night on some theory that I, a respected merchant, committed terrible crimes!'' the man said angrily. ''It is time for you to leave.''

The accusers exchanged frustrated glances.

''Wait! I have proof!'' said Marie suddenly. ''But we must have ink and more light!'' Her family and friends looked at her in astonishment.

The gentleman paused. ''Very well. I have nothing else to hide. Let us settle this matter now—and then I shall expect an apology from each and every one of you.'' He let loose his wife's hand for the first time since they'd entered the room. ''We'll go to my study.''

They entered a small room, crammed with correspondence. A small pot of ink stood on the table, beside a quill pen and sealing wax. Jacques, no less than any of the others, waited to see what Marie would do next.

She pulled the kidnapper's note out of her pouch and placed it on the table. ''There is a thumbprint clearly visible on the edge of the parchment where the ink was smeared,'' she said.

''Thumbprint'? What in the world is a 'thumbprint'?'' exclaimed Monsieur Dupuis.

She sighed heavily and plunged in. ''Our fingerprints

identify us. The little swirls on our fingers are unlike those on anyone else. By comparing the prints of your fingers, monsieur, with this one of the paper, we will know if you wrote the note.''

"Preposterous!" scoffed the merchant. "Fingers are just fingers. I'm not going to get my hands filthy, in the middle of the night, on your say-so. I've never heard of such a thing!''

Jacques came to her defense. "It's not a well-known idea, that's true. But all scribes know it, don't they, Father?''

"Well . . . of course they do," said Philippe, who was, in fact, completely in the dark.

"Yes," said Jacques. "We work with our fingers and ink all day long. So scribes have known for many years that fingerprints are a way to identify people. It's a secret of our guild." Marie gave him a grateful glance.

"Well, I don't believe it," snorted Monsieur Dupuis. "I'm certain that everyone here has exactly the same 'prints' on their fingers. So if you stick *my* thumbs in my ink, you'll stick everyone's, *including your own*!"

"All right," agreed Marie calmly. "I can live with that. But you go first."

So each of those present then dipped a thumb in the ink and pressed it to the parchment. Jacques picked up the sheet, and he and Marie studied it in the torchlight. They both gasped.

"Please, look here." Jacques held the parchment out to Monsieur Dupuis and Philippe. Madame Dupuis, Antonio, François, and even Benjamin, crowded around.

"Hmm. There *is* a match," muttered Monsieur Dupuis incredulously. He slowly turned his head. "It's . . . yours, Benjamin."

Benjamin's eyes were wide open, and all at once he looked like a trapped animal. Still, he shook his head. "That's absurd!" he snapped; then added, as an after-thought, "If you don't mind my saying so, sir."

"You're no servant," said Jacques. "You're the leader of the cult!"

"No. It's not true," answered Benjamin, but his words were undercut by the half-step backward he took.

"You told me you were in the East, where they know more about glass and mirrors!" said Marie.

"Just like your master, *you* saw the sketches for the manuscript when I brought them here for approval!" said Philippe.

"You drive a cart, and the kidnapper would need a cart to carry my father and Henri to the cave," said Jacques.

"No!" Benjamin said again. But before another charge could be hurled, he spun on his heel and raced down the hall toward the garden.

Jacques and Marie were both after him in a flash, leaving their elders gaping. The boy, so familiar with life on the soccer field, darted past his sister, and closed in on Benjamin like a greyhound. With a flying leap, he tackled the servant, throwing him into the thorny rosebush. They rolled free, the older man shouting at the pain of a dozen punctures, but fighting all the harder because of them. He kicked out at Jacques, knocking the boy backward. He started to get to his feet, but Marie slammed him across the back of the head with Madame Dupuis's distaff.

106

Monsieur Dupuis, Philippe, and Antonio found some rope to help Jacques restrain the man, while Madame Dupuis and the others went off to search Benjamin's room. They returned in triumph five minutes later.

"Look what we found hidden in his clothing chest," Marie said, and she held out the bowl of sparkling gems.

"This, too." Henri displayed the missing manuscript pages.

"And this," added Madame Dupuis, exhibiting a box full of golden necklaces and other fine jewelry.

Antonio took a closer look at that last item. With trembling hands he removed a large sapphire brooch from the box.

"This was my mother's family heirloom." He turned it over. "See here. It was inscribed on the back by my great-grandfather."

Antonio glared at Benjamin, who lay trussed up and truculent. "You tricked my father and many others in my town. You tried to trick the leaders of this town. But now, at last, you will pay for all your evil!"

Monsieur Dupuis went to change his clothes. When he came back, he said, "Please accompany me to the castle, Monsieur Fouché—you and your family. We shall return the jewels and clear your name."

Nineteen

DAWN WAS JUST BEGINNING TO LIGHTEN THE SKY AS PHIL-ippe, Jacques, and Marie returned to their home. Henri had invited Antonio to have a meal with him and François, followed by a good rest. The group planned to meet again that evening to discuss their amazing adventure.

Philippe held open the door as Marie and Jacques entered the scriptorium. The twins came to a halt inside and waited for him to close the door. When he looked up at them, their eyes were locked on him.

He smiled. "All right," he said, nodding sagely. "Come with me."

The twins followed silently as he led the way up the stairs to the bedrooms, then up the final stairs they'd been told never to use. He pulled out a key from under his tunic, which he kept on a cord around his neck, and unlocked the door at the top.

"Welcome to my second workshop, children," he said. "As you have guessed, I am not only a scribe."

A small table sat in the exact center of the room.

Surrounding it on the floor was a brightly colored circle with strange but beautifully calligraphed symbols. Nine unlit candles were arranged around that circle. Atop the table were a wand, a sword, a lamp, a cup, a bell, a small vial of fragrant oil, and an ancient book. Small clay containers were lined up on several shelves within easy reach. Philippe reached up to the ceiling and slid open a wooden shutter to expose the disappearing stars of the early morning sky above.

"Lemon juice, shavings of copper, mercury . . ." Jacques read the calligraphed labels indicating the contents of the pots. These labels were beautifully inscribed in Latin, but once again he had no trouble reading a foreign language. He fingered the balance scale that was placed on a second shelf next to the funnels and strainers.

"It reminds me of the chemistry lab at school," he said, looking at Philippe. A nod from the man confirmed that he understood.

"Yes, I know who you are," said their "father." "Or rather, who you are *not*!" Philippe thoughtfully stroked his beard as he looked from one of his descendants to the other.

"Now I will tell you how you arrived here," he said. "I am an alchemist, a sort of a magician, though not the sort Benjamin said I was! Most people, if they know of alchemy at all, think it involves turning lead or copper into gold. Some believe that if this secret of transmutation, as it is called, is learned, the secret to immortality will also be learned. They think there is a connection because of the long-lasting, or 'immortal,' quality of gold."

"I've learned that the work of the early alchemists helped develop the science of chemistry as we know it, but what does that have to do with our being here?" asked Jacques.

"All in good time, my . . . son," replied Philippe. He picked up one of the books from the stack in the corner. "My work as a scribe has enabled me to study many ancient manuscripts.

"This book is from Greece, and it is very old. I spent many years translating it and discovered a form of magic known only to a few others, throughout all of history. With this magic, I have been able to work a form of immortality, of which you twins are a part."

"This certainly is powerful magic to have brought us back nearly seven hundred years," exclaimed Marie. "But it seems to be immortality in the wrong direction!"

"It may seem that way to you," said Philippe, "but every thread, including the thread that runs through our family, has two ends, and connects all the points in between. You can come backward, and then go forward; it doesn't matter once the connection is made. My purpose was to harness that connection among all of the twins of our family line, past and future, with the hope that it could bring help in times of great need. Such a time was now, when only your knowledge from the future was able to solve Benjamin's crimes."

"In our time, we call that genetic connection—that thread—our DNA," said Jacques. "I couldn't tell you what those initials stand for—"

"I can," said Marie promptly. "It's *DeoxyriboNucleic Acid,* and it's the molecular basis for heredity.

Each person's DNA mixes with his partner's to create their children's DNA . . . so *your* DNA, Father—Philippe—is still in *us,* seven hundred years later. But what *I* want to know is, *why* did you choose us?" Marie asked. "Why not our twin aunts, or any of the other sets of twins anywhere in our family history?"

"Ah, now that's why they call it magic, and not science," replied Philippe with an almost embarrassed smile. "If one goes fishing, one may catch a fish, but no one can say *which* fish. All I could do was create the line, the connection, and then wait to see what it would bring me.

"You see, I knew I was in danger from the sect. Everything I told you in the cave was true, but what I didn't tell you was that I expected to be kidnapped—if not worse—after asking too many questions. So I 'sent' for twins from the future to act as detectives. I love my own Jacques and Marie, but I've kept them as ignorant of my alchemical workings as everyone else in town, and of course, they know nothing of 'fingerprints.' Not that I knew that fingerprints would solve the mystery, but I knew that my own twins definitely lacked the knowledge to do it. The odds were far better that twins from my future could, and I had little recourse but to throw out my line and hope I could catch two fish who could save both me and my town."

"But why didn't you just tell us what you wanted? You must have known who we were from the moment we arrived," Jacques said, and Marie nodded her agreement.

"As I say, alchemy is not science—not yet. I knew I'd captured my descendants, but I'm not foolish enough to think that all my descendants will be saints. I've kept the secret of my alchemical studies for a long time; I couldn't just announce it to you, in case you were of a mind to betray me. So I kept silent, but pushed you in certain directions—the middle folio of the manuscript, the theft of Henri's silver. If you were what I hoped you'd be, you'd be able to follow my clues. If you weren't . . . well, I was no worse off than I had been.''

Philippe embraced his young descendants. ''But you were everything I hoped you would be. You not only saved my life and the life of this town—you've given me the greatest gift a man can have: The certain knowledge that the future is bright.'' He stepped back but kept one hand on Jacques's shoulder and the other on Marie's. ''It has been a great pleasure to meet you both, my little fishes, but you must return now to your own parents. And, of course, my own Marie and Jacques must now return to me.''

''Where have they been?'' asked Jacques quickly, suddenly seeing the end of their adventure looming before him.

''Someplace safe, where time does not pass. Someplace much like sleep.''

''Won't they be confused when Henri and the others talk to them about what happened?'' Marie asked.

''No, they will feel as if they experienced it themselves, just as you were familiar with their habits and work. You and they remain connected through this . . . DNA,'' answered Philippe. ''My children may not be able to fully understand the future ideas you presented. For example, they will remember the flying machines as toy angels and the fingerprints as a game they had played with ink in the scriptorium. But they will remember.''

From under the table, Philippe brought out the magnificent book of the family tree, much shinier than when the twins had seen it last, in their own time. He opened it in the middle to the listing of his own family, the final entry thus far. Many blank pages followed, but as the twins knew, these would be faithfully filled out in the years to come. In the margin was the freshly written magic spell.

''Say it now . . . again,'' said Philippe Fouché.

Jacques and Marie took one long, last look at each other—as Jacques and Marie. Then they began to recite, and as they did so, they saw the familiar cloud of silver light, which faded to red, which spiraled around them and *clung* to them. And then . . .

Twenty

MRREŌWWWW, PURRED SCUBA, RUBBING AGAINST MARY'S ankles. The girl reached down to hug her kitten, and then just sat right down on the floor. *Her* floor, in *her* apartment. The scriptorium was home, but this was *home*!

"Ooh, I've missed you, you furry little *Felis domesticus*," she said fervently to the cat, who looked at her like "What's up with this?" but accepted the attention. Mary grinned at Jack, who nodded slowly back at her.

"Yeah, it's good to be home. Good to be talking English again." He looked at his wrist and the digital watch. "It's still Monday, and it's not even dinnertime yet!" he exclaimed in shocked tones.

"So no time has passed here, just like it didn't for Jacques and Marie. Amazing!" Mary said. Then, hesitatingly: "Jack—did it really happen?"

Her brother nodded firmly. "It really did, sis."

She let that sink in. . . . "All right, then. That's settled. It really happened. . . ." She jumped back to her feet.

114

"But Jack, we should keep quiet about it. It would worry Mom and Dad."

"Dad would want to know, sis. Being a historian and all . . ."

"He's still a dad. He and Mom worry if we stay out too late. If we told them we'd been fighting a crook in a cave in medieval France, or you were thrown in a pit with rats—"

"Yeah, yeah, yeah. You're right. The best we could hope for is they'd think we were nuts," replied Jack. "But, man, what a fantastic experience!"

"Com buer fumes nez!" laughed his sister, flopping into an overstuffed chair. " 'How fortunate we are!' See what a great French accent I have! My teacher will be so impressed."

"Your French is fourteenth-century French, sis. Talk like that and you'll pull an *F*! But when it comes to impressing a teacher, I think my problem with my history report is solved," responded Jack with a gleeful grin. "How's this for a title? 'The Life of a Scribe in the Middle Ages.' "

"Great! You'll ace that report for sure!" enthused Mary. "You—"

Suddenly she leapt to her feet and dashed over to the book of the family tree. It was still open to the page with the spell on it—the page of Philippe and Isabelle and Jacques and Marie. She studied it for a quick moment, and a huge smile lit up her face. "Marie and Antonio were married five years later, in 1318, and they had eight children! Eight children! It's so romantic!"

"Eight children is romantic?" exclaimed Jack, but he knew exactly what she meant. He'd liked Antonio—

115

though why anybody would want to marry Mary, in whatever era. . . . (On the other hand, he'd have to take a peek to see whom Jacques ended up with, sometime when Mary was nowhere around. Josiane *was* cute. . . .) "I guess that means you didn't have to worry about getting back here by Friday for your run with Allan Grant."

Mary gave him a pitying stare. "You really are nuts, bro. I'm glad to know that things worked out for Marie in the past, but *my* future's still bright!"

"Yeah, yeah, sis," said her twin. "And now that the past is open to us, there's no telling just how bright our future can *get*. . . ."

Join in the Wild and Crazy Adventures with Some Trouble-Making Plants

by Nancy McArthur

THE PLANT THAT ATE DIRTY SOCKS
75493-2/ $4.50 US/ $5.99 Can

THE RETURN OF THE PLANT THAT ATE DIRTY SOCKS
75873-3/ $3.99 US/ $5.50 Can

THE ESCAPE OF THE PLANT THAT ATE DIRTY SOCKS
76756-2/ $3.50 US/ $4.25 Can

THE SECRET OF THE PLANT THAT ATE DIRTY SOCKS
76757-0/ $3.99 US/ $4.99 Can

MORE ADVENTURES OF THE PLANT THAT ATE DIRTY SOCKS
77663-4/ $3.99 US/ $4.99 Can

THE PLANT THAT ATE DIRTY SOCKS GOES UP IN SPACE
77664-2/ $3.99 US/ $5.50 Can

THE MYSTERY OF THE PLANT THAT ATE DIRTY SOCKS
78318-5/ $3.99 US/ $4.99 Can

IF YOU DARE TO BE SCARED...
READ SPINETINGLERS!
by M.T. COFFIN